ROSIE JACKSON

THE
PEACE
PARABLES

HOW THE FOOL BECAME GOD
AND OTHER STORIES

This book is dedicated to all those who,

In their own unique ways,

contribute to the creation of a

peaceful world

Rosie Jackson

ART by Rosie Jackson: www.rosiejackson.de

Bibliografische Information der Deutschen Nationalbibliothek:
Die Deutsche Nationalbibliothek verzeichnet diese Publikation
in der Deutschen Nationalbibliografie; detaillierte bibliografische
Daten sind im Internet über http://dnb.dnb.de abrufbar.

Herstellung und Verlag: BoD – Books on Demand, Norderstedt

Erste Auflage Januar 2020

ISBN: 9783750441514

TABLE OF CONTENTS

Introduction

This book contains 56 "peace parables". Most of these are visions received during meditation between 2009 and 2019. Readers who are unfamiliar with this process may ask "How do these visions arise?". We need to sit in a quiet place, close our eyes, breathe deeply, clear our minds and ask our questions with sincere intent. The answer will appear in our "mind's eye", perhaps as words, colours, feelings, or pictures. This is a transmission from our "divine fragment within" which is an experienced and wise advisor. As I am also an artist, answers to my questions during meditation tend to appear in the form of visuals and stories. Following meditation, I write down what I have seen.

A few of the parables are adaptations of messages which I have received telepathically from Seraphin. Seraphin is an angel who has been the inspiration behind much of my creative work since 2009. A selection of his most poignant messages has been published in SERAPHIN'S SPIRITUALITY SCHOOL (2019, Rosie Jackson).

The Power of Words

The title of this book is taken from the longest parable called HOW THE FOOL BECAME GOD. A fool is someone whose "foolish" thoughts and actions cause unfortunate situations. Fools have not fully realised that their present words actually form their future reality. In a way, we are all FOOLS, always in the process of learning. At the same time, we are all GODDESSES and GODS who teach during our every encounter.

Utterances such as I WILL NEVER BE ANY GOOD AT THIS or THINGS ALWAYS TURN OUT WRONG FOR ME are self-fulfilling prophecies. If we want to empower ourselves, we are invited to choose our words with ultimate care so that they attract positive experiences.

The Goddess in HOW THE FOOL BECAME GOD says the following about words:

"Weigh every word for its relevance and beauty before you sound it publically. Consider its effect and its longevity, or whether it is chaff which will simply blow away in wind. Chose words which lend wings to your listeners. Avoid words which hammer your listeners into silence. Disregard words which you repeat constantly but which fail to penetrate conflicted, dense or stagnant minds. Discard all words which rebound without success. And when there is no hope of being heard, be still."

Words are of utmost importance. We can train ourselves to increase awareness of what we say. For example, we can record our conversations and review them later. Or we can spend a day blindfold, cutting ourselves off from all visual distractions and forcing ourselves to focus on sound. This vastly amplifies our perception of hesitance, ambiguity and aggression in spoken language. We quickly perceive what is relevant, and what is incoherent, superfluous babble.

This applies not only to words, but to the thoughts which precede our words. In fact, everything counts. We can learn to choose our thoughts – and thus the reality we manifest as a result - with care, discernment and confidence, creating the highest good for all. Once "fools" have understood that their choice of words and actions can benefit humanity, and act upon this knowledge, they will become "gods".

Peace through Parables

The "peace parables" are so named because they are intended to assist the development of peace on this world. Peace can be achieved through increased and continuous awareness of our behaviour and potential, if directed towards the common good. These parables illustrate which behaviours fit into this category, and which do not.

All the stories are designed to assist readers on their spiritual journey, opening up new vistas, opportunities and directions. The stories provide insights, shake up superstitions, encourage heroic acts, warn against stagnation, expose corruption, break slave mentalities, revive creative powers, invite reassessment, reveal downward spirals, inspire love of nature, destroy debilitating dependence, discourage materialism, denounce arrogance and foster true values

The stories also urge us to search for better solutions, clarify our choices, increase compassion and recognise our interconnection. They illuminate dangerous domino effects, exposing narrowmindedness and blind allegiance. Most importantly, the stories show us "another way", preparing us to be flexible in the face of great change, and forcing us to reflect upon that which is of supreme importance - our life's purpose.

The Power of Parables

Parables are an excellent way of teaching, as they entertain and educate people of various paths, without raising an accusing finger. No one is addressed personally. It is up to readers to draw their own conclusions. One of the most famous storytellers is the soul we call Jesus, and the following discussion on parables with his disciples is a fine summary of their potential:

"The apostles were parable-minded, so much so that the whole of the next evening was devoted to the further discussion of parables. Jesus introduced the evening's conference by saying: "My beloved, you must always make a difference in teaching so as to suit your presentation of truth to the minds and hearts before you. When you stand before a multitude of varying intellects and temperaments, you cannot speak different words for each class of hearers, but you can tell a story to convey your teaching; and each group, even each individual, will be able to make his own interpretation of your parable in accordance with his own intellectual and spiritual endowments (…)

The parable provides for a simultaneous appeal to vastly different levels of mind and spirit. The parable stimulates the imagination, challenges the discrimination, and provokes critical thinking; it promotes sympathy without arousing antagonism.

The parable proceeds from the things which are known to the discernment of the unknown. The parable utilizes the material and natural as a means of introducing the spiritual and the supermaterial.

Parables favor the making of impartial moral decisions. The parable evades much prejudice and puts new truth gracefully into the mind and does all this with the arousal of a minimum of the self-defense of personal resentment.

To reject the truth contained in parabolical analogy requires conscious intellectual action which is directly in contempt of one's honest judgment and fair decision. The parable conduces to the forcing of thought through the sense of hearing.

The use of the parable form of teaching enables the teacher to present new and even startling truths while at the same time he largely avoids all controversy and outward clashing with tradition and established authority.

The parable also possesses the advantage of stimulating the memory of the truth taught when the same familiar scenes are subsequently encountered.

In this way Jesus sought to acquaint his followers with many of the reasons underlying his practice of increasingly using parables in his public teaching."

From *Paper 151: Tarrying and Teaching at the Seaside, The Urantia Book*

Thank you for reading. May these parables reach the parts of you which require reassessment, and may we all fulfil our mandate, which is to manifest godliness and peace on this earth.

Rosie Jackson, January 2020

CHAPTER 1

PARABLES
WHICH TEACH
WHO WE REALLY ARE

HOW THE FOOL BECAME GOD

The Fool stated firmly: "I WILL NOT GET OUT OF BED UNTIL I SEE THE SUN", and thus saying, he turned over and hid beneath the covers. Seeing his great disappointment, the Goddess replied: "Rise and walk outside in the meadows in the full knowledge of your divinity and your eternal inner sun, and then the clouds shall part."

The Fool admitted: "THAT WOMAN IN HIGH HEELS IS TURNING MY HEAD", and thus saying, his eyes followed her body as she swayed across the floor. The Goddess replied: "If your heart has been turned on, if your sincerity has deepened, if your dedication has been fired, then truly the shoes play little part in this."

The Fool complained: "THE OVEN IS COLD", and the Goddess replied: "If you always extend full awareness to the flames, you will place wood into the furnace the moment the fire shows signs of dying. You will feel miniscule changes in the warmth's intensity so acutely that even a fleeting and momentary lull will pierce you like a sword, causing you to investigate the reason. You will immediately leap into action. And in this way, the fire will never die and you will never encounter the disappointment of a cold unwelcoming hearth".

The Fool lamented: "I CANNOT DANCE", but the Goddess advised him: "Pay attention to support and balance continuously. Do not stand so firm that the music cannot move you. Do not stand so weak that you are supplanted by the first flow of soft water. Remain rooted, but be prepared to uproot immediately as the situation or the tune demands. Prefer flexibility to the brittle stance of stubbornness. Prefer to run with the wind, to battling the storm. Meander like the river, rather than circle the same pivot repeatedly. Having practiced all this, you will have danced."

The Fool sighed: "MY GARDEN IS FULL OF BRIARS", and the Goddess suggested: "Attend to your soil regularly. Avoid *tabula rasa*: do not destroy everything to clear a space, for in doing so, you will destroy not only the briars but also the flowers which inspire you with their beauty. You will maim the corn which provides your food. Extract carefully that which offends, and nurture that which you cherish. Discover the fruits which lie hidden beneath the undergrowth. Thus shall your garden path be girded with beauty.

The Fool complained "I AM AS POOR AS A CHURCH MOUSE", and the Goddess replied: "Consider your words carefully before you place them in the public arena, for they grow with attention and accumulate power whenever expressed. Repetition consolidates. Comparisons belittle you and keep you in a state of dearth. Turn your gaze instead towards abundance in all its forms: abundance of air, abundance of interesting encounters, abundance of laughter, abundance of dance and abundance of song. And when you are fully drenched in this abundance, you will be DRUNKEN WITH THE DIVINE and wealthy beyond belief."

The Fool put his hands over his ears screaming "THE NOISE IS TOO LOUD", and the Goddess recommended: "Seek places of stillness where you are graced with silence. Drink your fill until you are a pool of serenity, remaining calm however many stones are thrown rudely into your waters. Then can you enter all doors beyond which chaos reigns.

The Fool cried: "MY THROAT IS SORE", and the Goddess replied: "Show restraint in your replies. Weigh every word for its relevance and beauty before you sound it publically. Consider its effect and its longevity, or whether it is chaff which will simply blow away in wind. Chose words which lend wings to your listeners. Avoid words which hammer your listeners into silence. Disregard words which you repeat constantly but which fail to penetrate conflicted, dense or stagnant minds. Discard all words which rebound without success. And when there is no hope of being heard, be still. Then your voice will not be cracked or strained, but smooth and relaxed."

The fool exclaimed: "MY HANDS ARE NUMB", and the Goddess replied: "Rub your hands together and feel the warmth you are able to generate. Through friction and encounter with others, you may initiate motion in heart and mind. Your actions will take you further along a road where others travel also. You may offer to carry their luggage for a while. You may make them tea or hold their hand. When you connect in this way, the energy in your hands will not remain in cold stagnation, but will be transferred to another, forming a circuit, forming a whole. Then your hands will feel alive".

The Fool sobbed: "I AM DULL AND OVERLOOKED", and the Goddess replied: "Survey the colours of your inspiration and talents. If your song is blue, do not sing against a blue wall. If your script is yellow, do not write on yellow paper. If your love is red, do not walk upon a red carpet. Clarify your purpose, sharpen your focus and risk stepping into the light. Show openly your song, your script and your love to everyone you meet. Then you will be seen completely"

The Fool complained: "I HAVE LITTLE BRAIN. THERE IS SO MUCH I DO NOT UNDERSTAND", and the Goddess replied: "Regard the bee which gingerly treads the delicate petals of the dandelion in search of nectar. Regard the tiny ants who know exactly where to go and how to build a home in unison. And then turn your gaze from these microcosms to the macrocosms – to the stars all around you, and know that each pin prink of light may be a universe. If you can recognise the intricate design of this, if you can marvel at the growth of a leaf, if you can conceive of the power behind your breath when you sleep, if you can see the energy behind the mystery, if you can wonder at the glory of the Divine Hand, THEN YOU WILL HAVE UNDERSTOOD ALL."

The Fool sighed: " I AM ABANDONED AND ALONE", and the Goddess replied: "If you greet each being as a brother or sister, if you peer through the shadows of sorrow to the rushing rivers of life beyond, if you uphold the image of a timeless zone where all encounters play out in the NOW, if you raise your eyes in great expectation to the light, in awareness of the next great gift to be bestowed on thee, if you open your arms and heart to all those who cross your path, if you move with hope and gratitude, if you recognise the subtle trait of guiding godliness as a constant in your life, THEN YOU WILL NEVER BE ALONE".

The Fool said: I STAND FALSELY ACCUSED", and the Goddess replied: "To accuse someone is to point your finger and find the fault in them which you recognise. You can only recognise something which is in yourself. Thus, any accusation YOU make of another, whether "true" or "false", IT WILL BE TRUE OF YOURSELF. Similarly; anyone who accuses you is looking into their own mirror, as you constantly do also. Recognise your errors with the aid of the mirror. Polish the surface so that its reflection is constantly clear and shining, so that the learning process ABOUT YOURSELF can progress as the fastest pace. The mirror will be your best teacher. The behaviour of others will show you facets of your own behaviour for your own scrutiny. In this way, no one can accuse you, because YOU HAVE BECOME YOUR OWN JUDGE.

The Fool lamented: THE RIVER HAS SWEPT MY BOAT AWAY", and the Goddess replied: "If you learn to observe the force of the wind, the pull of the moon, the melting of the snows and the strength of the sun, you may see the effect on ebb and flow, on speed and volume, on height and depth, on vibration in all its manifested forms. And in the end, you will be so familiar with continual change that your wise assessments will quash the breeding ground of disappointment.

The Fool said: "I HAVE BEEN THROWN OUT OF MY HOME", and the Goddess said: "Home is the space around and inside yourself where you feel at rest and content. This can be any-where, yet your "home space" around you feels familiar. You hes-itate before you allow strangers or new things to enter this space, but what is the source of this hesitation? If you overcome it and welcome all instantly and spontaneously, all can enter, and your home expands to incorporate all. Thus, HOME IS EVERY-WHERE.

The Fool said "I AM ILL", and the Goddess replied: "Illness is the effect of ill-chosen decisions manifested – from actions too hasty, too ponderous, too disparate or too narrow. You may be moti-vated by inappropriate goals or subversive aims. Your moves may be incomplete, unclear or misdirected, thus harming others and SELF, over-exposing and over-straining already inherent weaknesses which develop into full-blown blockages or PAIN. To avoid this, aspire to honesty, translucency and directness, al-ways readjusting your actions and reactions so they overlook nothing and address ALL.

The Fool said: "I AM TIRED AND IMPATIENT", and the Goddess replied: "If you observe the regular and unforced pattern of na-ture, the way leaves fall when they are dry, the way fruit ripens at exactly the right moment to nourish the seed, the way hibernating animals are awakened by exactly the right temperature for their new phase of life, you will realise that these regulative measures apply to your own awakening and growth also. The more you push issues, relationships or deadlines, the more tired you be-come. The further you deviate from nature's laws, the more ten-sion you will develop in your progression against them. Know that you are assisted at all crossroads by the signs of Divine Hand. If you act in conscious alignment with these, you will travel easily and be light of heart, pacing yourself according to Divine Design, knowing everything ripens at the ideal moment. Thus, fatigue and impatience disappear from your mental landscape.

The Fool said: "I AM AFRAID", and the Goddess answered: "Fear is WORRYING IN ADVANCE OF MANIFESTATION. It is a presumption about something which has not yet happened, incited and coloured by previous losses or sadness. You think the same is going to happen again. But this is in the past. It is irrelevant to the NOW, the NOT YET FUTURE, THE BLANK PAGE which has yet to be written upon. You chose your pen, you chose the moment when you write, you describe the nature of your experience in the language of your choice. If you fuse your pen with the ink of fear, you will write shakily and unclearly. If you write with the ink of openness and determination, you will trace a script with firm contours and weighed import. Thus will you always be able to write with confidence".

The Fool said: "MY DREAMS NEVER COME TRUE", and the Goddess replied: "To have a vision of a better future for yourself and your fellow companions is a worthy aim. To see and implement the potential in a less than perfect situation is to advance and ride on the edge of history in the making. However, it is irresponsible to ignore the changing direction of the trade winds, the leaks in the boat and the sharks in the water. Investigate your terrain, secure all holes, know your companions and set your course. Make land stops, recuperating, reorienting and buying provisions as necessary. And if there is a new map, do not persist in using an old one. Keep the object of your vision in view at all times, for it still exists though you may make detours or sail through storms to get there. Make the journey a series of successful stages rather than one long voyage which daunts you into resignation when you survey it from the shore at your starting point. If you exercise all this, YOUR DREAMS WILL COME TRUE.

The Fool stated: I AM NO ONE, UNLESS I WEAR THE CLOTHES OF A KING", and the Goddess answered: "To initiate long-term respect, effort to understand that the degree of purity you demonstrate is paramount. If your motives are besmirched, so will the results of your actions be besmirched. If you feed your crops with poisoned water, they will fail you. If you feed your relationships with false promises, they will founder. If you wear a mask, the reactions you provoke are reactions to the mask and not to your true self. If you blow a favourable, gentle, humid wind, the leaves will dance and your orchard will flourish. If you blow a royal trumpet to announce instant, uncompromising, infallible decrees, without true knowledge of the conditions of your kingdom, your trees will fail to bring fruit. If you wear the clothes of a pauper but can connect with the hearts of all, you will be king."

The Fool hung his head and said "FROM YOUR WORDS OF WISDOM, I CAN SEE THAT I AM JUST A FOOL", and the Goddess replied: "Those who recognise that there is more to understand will continue their search for the truth. Such seekers use every opportunity to learn, and having accumulated knowledge, they automatically attract those who wish to learn also. Thus, they become teachers. And because they continue to learn, their teaching capacity expands eternally, until they reach the highest level."

The Fool whispered "BUT I COULD NEVER BE LIKE GOD", and the Goddess replied: "If you already know what God could be like, how can you not grow towards that image? If you can imagine divine grace in eternity, what limits are there to your imagination? If you can express the frustration of limitation, your eye can travel towards the endless horizon, the residence of the Divine, from whence you then return to see the Divine in all things, IN-CLUDING IN YOURSELF AS GOD". Then the Fool put his hand in the hand of the Goddess and wept. And then he smiled, and wept again. And she continued to teach him, and he continued to teach her how to teach, and thus they continued to walk, and to part, and to walk together again, until finally they met on the endless horizon and returned.

TWELVE DISCIPLES DISCOVER THE DIVINE WITHIN

Once upon a time there was a group of twelve friends who worked during the day and met at night. They were young, rebellious, reckless and yearned for freedom. They spurned old rituals, conventional expectations and limiting ideas. They travelled fast, pushing everything aside to find the next stimulus, the next laugh, the next ride before returning to their daily routine. Life was a series of extreme highs and extreme lows, and they urged each other on until they were all weary, depressed, addicted and "burnt out". But their hearts were still burning, bearing a flame of hope that one day, they would find another way.

They instinctively knew that this day had arrived when, during intense wanderings (and intense wanderings of the soul) they discovered a sign saying NO ENTRY: DANGER. In this lonely and desecrated place, they felt that they had reached the end of the world. Beyond the sign lay a very high wall. It was obvious that some people had already attempted to climb it, for old ladders lay rotting on the ground.

As the twelve cautiously moved past the sign towards the wall, they heard various faint sounds in the distance – bells tinkling, flutes playing, voices singing and praying, trees swaying, feet dancing, wings flapping, animals slithering through grass, book pages turning, people breathing, and silence.

But the sounds picked up by the twelve were not always the same. Their inner "antennae" picked up the sound which attracted them most. It was almost as if one special sound was calling them saying THERE IS NO DANGER HERE: ENTER AND BE FREE. THIS IS YOUR CALLING. And the call was so strong that they ignored the sign and climbed the wall, to be greeted by a world so expansive, so strong and potent that it took their breath away. It was as if a GREAT SACRED STILLNESS suddenly poured into their troubled minds, allowing them to focus on THEIR TRUE NATURES and THEIR TRUE VOCATIONS.

One by one they searched the beautiful landscape for the origin of the sound which had entranced them – melodious flutes, snakes shedding their skin, trees rustling, the deep breathing of meditating monks, the flapping wings of iridescent butterflies, the tapping of feet. They heard sounds of singers and dancers who were all LIVING THEIR DREAM FULLY, ALL AWARE OF THEIR INNER STRENGTH, ALL CONNECTED TO THE DIVINE, ALL IN THE FULL KNOWLEDGE OF THEMSELVES AS GODS.

As the twelve disciples wandered through this paradise on the other side of the wall, they could easily have lost their way, but their ears were continually alive to the sounds, and their eyes were continually searching for signs to show them their very own sacred path - signs of harmony, wisdom, nurturing, life, balance, rebirth, transformation, growth, eternity, exuberance, abundance, dedication and love. The more signs they noted and followed, the more convinced they became that their direction was being managed by DIVINE ORCHESTRATION, and that their destination was similarly DIVINE.

They moved from one stage to the next, through twelve stages of spiritual development, which simultaneously caused 12 changes in their physical development. As their concept of all things possible expanded, they connected telepathically with other souls in their group, with angels, with entities in unseen realms and on other planets, until they realised that they were actually CONNECTED TO ONE GREAT DIVINE WHOLE. They also realised that a part of that Divine Whole RESIDED IN THEM.

As large, wise beings with hearts full of love, the twelve often looked over the wall in the direction of where they had come. They called it EARTH, and longed to take a piece of "HEAVEN" there to alleviate the pain of its inhabitants. They realised that this was their mandate – to strive until all earth resembled the garden which they had discovered beyond the wall. And so, they started to sing, read, dance, meditate and breathe, so that those on earth would have enough patterns, signs and DIVINE IN-STRUCTIONS to encourage them to climb the wall.

INSIDE THE MARBLE

A group of art students wandered through a large marble quarry, looking at all the blocks of marble and trying to decide which one to choose. Some took a long time over this, pondering the quality and size of the stones, and others selected intuitively and without hesitation. Those who took their time were gently ushered on by the master sculptor, who was supervising the whole operation. He gently reminded them that the outside form of the block of marble was not so important, and that it was the INSIDE which mattered.

The master sculptor then gave the students the task of DISCOV-ERING THEMSELVES. He told them that by chipping off the out-side layer of the marble, they would find an aspect of themselves which required more attention. So, everyone was given a hammer and chisel and was told to begin.

This was no easy work, as some had never held a hammer before, but as they experimented with dedication, they made progress and were very excited to find the first "unchipable" part of stone, which meant that they had found the tip of what they were looking for. Some did not really understand what this whole process was about. They tired quickly and laid down their tools from time to time, but they were inspired to continue when they saw that others had made headway.

Eventually, after many hours of excavation, nearly everyone had finished. A bell rang. The students sat in a long row opposite the object they had excavated, and were asked to contemplate what they had to learn.

One student sat opposite the head of an emperor, and this signified that his next task was to develop leadership qualities. Another student sat opposite the head of a cartoon-like dog, with a large tongue hanging out of its mouth, making it look rather ridiculous. This signified that the student should concentrate in more depth on developing his spiritual nature.

One woman, who had only managed to chip away half of her marble block, sat opposite the creased and twisted face of an angry witch, wearing a pointed hat. She could not come to terms with this at all and fell into a sorry heap, accusing the master sculptor of being hard-hearted. The master sculptor picked her up gently and handed her the hammer. He turned the marble block around and asked her to chip away at the other side.

It took her a very long time to do this, as she kept on breaking off to lament her dreadful situation, and to scream that the witch-like face had nothing to do with her. But the master sculptor urged her to continue, saying she must continue if she really wanted change. Finally, the other side of the witch's head was revealed – the face of a beautiful young woman. This signified that the woman was a goddess who had actually forgotten that she was a goddess.

LIBERATING THE PENAL COLONY

A group of people were meditating inside a huge circular compound at the centre of penal colony. The prisoners, all wearing identical clothes, paraded around this circular compound, as this was part of their daily "exercise". Some prisoners were so apathetic or felt so weak that it was very difficult to put one foot in front of the other. Their eyes were always cast upon the ground. Other prisoners were very alert, watching the others carefully with darting roving eyes to discover any differences. They would see immediately if one prisoner was fatter than another, which meant that they were receiving secret rations, and they would see immediately whether anyone had shoes in better condition than their own, and they would then switch pairs at an opportune moment. They were on the look-out for anything which could be stolen. Yet other prisoners regarded their fellow inmates with compassion, not seeking anything for themselves but assessing how they could best give.

There were very few prisoners who – in addition to being aware of themselves and others – were also aware of the fact THAT THEY WERE NOT WALKING IN A STRAIGHT LINE. The few that also kept their eyes ON THE SUN AND ITS POSITION understood that they must be walking in a circle, ending up at the same place that they began. Some realised that there MUST BE SOMETHING BEHIND THE WALL AND WITHIN THAT CIRCLE, but most prisoners did not realise, and indeed, they rarely looked up at all.

For those who did look up one cold night, a sudden light met their eyes. The light began as a dull glow above the rim of the wall, and then it became a huge flame which was startling in its intensity. In a flash, it started to explode, and small round golden objects fell to the ground, landing at the feet of the prisoners. All the prisoners stopped in their tracks immediately. Some prisoners recognised this as money and fell on their knees, pushing others aside in their scramble to collect it. But as they did so, the golden "coins" slipped through their fingers. This was not actually solid metal but a feathery, stretchy material which floated everywhere and glinted fabulously.

Other prisoners watched in wonder as tall golden figures appeared before them. They started to gather the floating material and heaped it gently onto themselves, motioning to the prisoners to do the same. Those who regarded this scene in wonder and love, aware that a great transformation process was being initiated, started to gather the golden flakes which seemed to stick to their skin like magnets. It clung to their bodies until they were covered completely by a golden shroud. Those prisoners who harboured vicious and mercenary thoughts were not able to attract the golden particles and were led away.

Those prisoners who were usually quite friendly but who kept themselves to themselves, meaning no harm, were very afraid. The golden flakes were not attracted to them, but neither did they disperse. When the tall golden beings opened the doors of the penal colony, they rushed out to find their families.

Then the golden figures took the hands of the remaining prisoners, who were now wearing shrouds of gold, and led them to the top of a nearby hill. From this vantage point, it was clear that there were actually THOUSANDS OF PEOPLE who had completed this process of BECOMING LIGHT, for golden-clad beings lined the ridges of all mountains, as far as the eye could see.

People in the valleys looked into the skies and saw a flurry of very unusual activity. They saw "stars" which moved, and this plunged them all into great fear. The presence of the still, golden lights on the mountains, however, were a source of great consolation and hope.

After some time, all the golden-clad beings walked down the mountains into the villages, and the villagers recognised the former prisoners. This was cause for great rejoicing, and it completely eliminated the fear which had afflicted them previously. Thus, the gold-clad beings were able to speak their truth and were accepted as messengers of a new and better way of living.

FINDING THE WATERFALL OF TRUTH

Due to a sense of great crisis, a group of riders on horses were riding AS FAST AS POSSIBLE on a very vital mission. They all wore armour and carried spears and banners. Together they formed a very colourful crowd, as they came from many different races and tribes. Even the horses were various surprising shades of colour, apart from the normal black or brown. All together they raced on, leaving clouds of dust and darkness behind them, searching valiantly for the only thing which still interested them – THE WATERFALL OF TRUTH.

As they travelled on, the valley became increasingly narrow, and the sides became steeper, forcing the riders to bunch together. In addition, they were aware that other riders had joined them on the way, but they did not know exactly who these extra riders were because they were also wearing armour, and visors covered their faces. Their focus remained on the horizon, scanning it for the waterfall that they KNEW must be there, judging from the width of the river and the steepness of their ascent. They

KNEW that the valley ended and that the waterfall must become visible soon.

At last, they arrived at the waterfall, weary and thirsty, and they stopped and drank of its waters. Almost immediately, they RE-MEMBERED WHO THEY REALLY WERE – their true selves.

Then everyone took off their armour and started to recognise each other from other missions and past lives. Grand reunions took place. Everyone sat and talked about old times, knowing that the "veil of forgetfulness" had been lifted by their impassioned search for the waterfall of truth. They now knew that they would be working together always.

THE RUNNING MAN

A man is running along a road. The road stretches before him in a completely straight line, ending at a lighthouse in the far distance. He concentrates on moving forward with all his might, in order to reach his destination.

As he runs, his awareness is on the light at the top of the lighthouse, guiding his steps on a purely physical level. Yet he is also aware that the same steps, at different times, feel lighter or heavier. This is because the road, although perfectly straight, also rises and falls from time to time, although it is not perceptible to the eye.

As he runs through the night, his eyes see the light more clearly – an immobile pinpoint contrasting with the stars which move across the sky. And during the day, the light all but disappears, yet he knows it is there. As he runs, he reflects that the ground he is running on is actually a planet, turning through periods of night and day, and that the spinning planet is also moving round the sun.

As his thoughts turns inward, he reflects upon the constant circuit within himself, the passage of blood, the expelling of residue, the eternal renewal process of his cells, and he wonders in particular at the resilience of the cells on the soles of his feet which are under constant pressure. He notices his breath – regular when relaxed, flat when in fear, imperceptible when he is asleep. In periods of heightened awareness, he becomes the earth herself, imagining what it must be like to feel the imprint of his running shoes on her body, how they bend the grass, how they thud on the concrete which prevents her breath.

In the end, the running man reaches his destination and surveys the landscape from the top of the lighthouse, only to find that a new circle of potential destinations has opened up to him. Reflecting upon past and potential future journeys, he recognises the DENSITY of the physical matter he has traversed, and the physical body he has used to traverse it, but his experience has been so much more than this. NEW DIMENSIONS have opened up to him, resulting from his ability to reflect, observe, empathise and wonder. Holding all these perceptions at once, the running man recognises himself as part of the ENTIRE COSMOS AT ALL TIMES.

THE FOOL'S PROGRESS:
TAKING UP THE SPIRITUAL SWORD

The Fool said: "THERE ARE SO MANY WARS. HOW CAN I HOPE TO MAKE A DIFFERENCE?" and the Goddess answered: "You can straddle the divide, because you are a bridge between heaven and earth. Imagine a globe of intense light above you, and imagine the earth mapped below. With your inner eye, see all the places where RED is concentrated, for this is where blood is spilled, or where soldiers are trained to spill blood, or where weapons, tanks and ammunition are produced, or where chemicals, electronics and technology are developed to assist the spilling of blood. YET ALL THESE WOULD FALL INTO DISUSE AND DECAY IF THE INHABITANTS OF EARTH WERE FILLED WITH LOVE. This is your aim.

Focus upon the red areas. They may be military or civilian centres. They may be prominent or hidden. They may be visible or underground. They may be underwater or hovering above the atmosphere of the earth. Focus upon each in turn, drawing a thin red thread upwards and past yourself until it fuses with the globe of light above you. Continue until ALL RED AREAS ARE LINKED TO THE DIVINE LIGHT.

Then look up and see that the divinely lighted globe, in its turn, is linked by beams of white light to many other bright spheres throughout the universe and beyond. Know that this is a huge and infinitely powerful network. Inform all inhabitants on these spheres of your firm intent to transform all that is red to white, and request their assistance.

Synchronise and concentrate this huge energy by calling a countdown: 10, 9, 8, 7, 6, 5, 4, 3, 2, 1. On the count of 0, feel the joint energy cumulate and explode in the bright sphere above you. See it travel down the red threads attached to earth, and see it move in one united wall of absolute pure LOVE to cover the entire surface of the earth.

Imagine this map and initiate this process whenever you wish to go into action, and take up your spiritual sword.

WHAT THE FOOL NEEDED TO KNOW

The fool was despondent. He hung his head and said "I feel tired, alone, impatient, instable, unloved and directionless. What do I need to know to continue on my life's journey?" Then he closed his eyes and heard the answer to his question:

"If you are in a complex process, you need to know that IMPATIENCE IS MISPLACED. If everything happened smoothly and quickly, IT WOULD NOT BE A PROCESS, and no learning would be gleaned from that.

You need to know that impediments to your heart's desire will be eradicated by the force of your desire. You chose the pace. Either you chew off small pieces at regular intervals and digest them at leisure, or you bite off huge chunks when you are ravenous, but which have the effect of choking you. You need to practise CONTINUOUS ASSESSMENT of situations, instead of deciding THIS IS SO, and then leaving it for months in this state of stagnation. Unsolved issues are unsolved because they have not been addressed in good time.

You need to know that hopping on one leg makes for instability. Decide on basic principles and direct your life accordingly. Always steer your boat towards the rising sun, not towards the dying light. Fly your plane in the sunlight above the clouds. Do not fly through the thick of the storm. Rejoice in the infinite number of new worlds and experiences opening up towards you.

Set up a "calm room" in reality (or in your mind) where you can rest at regular intervals. Take a walk to feel stillness in your soul, to see things pass by while YOU remain the same.

Reach out to those who enter your circle, but do not allow them to become your pivot. Listen for changes and speak your truth. Carry tools with you constantly, like a bunch of keys, ever prepared to unlock a stubborn heart (including your own): use the key of compassion, the key of gentle enquiry, the key of honesty, the key of redressing balance, the key of retreat to let growth occur in another.

You need to know that love is never lost, and that its source is eternal. You need to know that unquenchable thirst will lead you to the deepest never-ending source. You need to know that pallid desire leads to a small puddle. You need to know that the distractions of this material world – centred on food, appearance, status and entertainment – are merely distractions. Know that beauty is everywhere, in every cell, including every cell of yourself. Know that love, laughter and enthusiasm are infectious.

You need to know that your view is necessarily limited, but rejoice that I your Creator have an ALL-SEEING EYE. Trust in my decisions which are based on a bird's eye view. Know that all aspects are always taken into account BECAUSE I SEE ALL. Be comforted that this is so, and that I love my children, taking every opportunity as a father does to support your learning process towards joyful independence. You need to know that many will face new experiences, will have to move to a new place, a new home, with new people. I say that these places, homes and people HAVE BEEN THERE ALL THE TIME, the only difference being your movement towards them and your awakening to their existence. And I say: I AM THE VOICE OF THE DIVINE WITHIN YOU: AWAKEN TO MY EXISTENCE, FOR I HAVE BEEN HERE ALL THE TIME."

CHAPTER 2

PARABLES
WHICH INVITE
US TO REASSESS

THE ROOF

There was once a concrete city with very few green areas, and the whole district was covered by a roof and sealed off from the exterior by thick walls. The inhabitants were small, stunted humans who stooped and walked slowly, their eyes turning to the ground in great humility, as if they recognised having committed a major crime and were doing everything in their power to make amends. And indeed, it was the general consensus that they HAD actually committed a crime of great proportions, for their leaders had built the roof over their heads to protect them from the air which had been polluted and poisoned by all sorts of human actions and waste products.

For this, all inhabitants were genuinely sorry. They realised that they had collectively destroyed "nature", and that it was now their responsibility to nurture it. Thus, everyone was greatly encouraged to look after a number of pot plants, sending them love every day. Those with knowledge about plants warned that these remaining species were also severely weakened, and that they would not survive strong exposure to light, and would suffer from over-watering and from repotting.

Sometimes the inhabitants would take their pot plants for a walk. If they wished to venerate their pot plants, they would take them to the GARDEN OF NATURE ADORATION where – it was felt – there was a higher vibration due to the accumulation of plants. At the very centre of the garden was the trunk of an enormous tree. The inhabitants were given to understand that the tree was now dead but that it had once been a flourishing example of "nature" in the old days, when everything was still intact and when the air was still pure.

Every day, people would pour into the garden bearing their pot plants, remembering the once glorious tree, admitting their guilt and stating their intent to make amends. They prayed and sang, determined to do their very best to rectify their wrong. They were determined to live humbly, with few possessions and demands, for the collective good. They praised and thanked their leaders for building the roof at a very critical period in their history so long ago, which had preserved their existence and which had avoided the complete obliteration of their species.

The huge tree trunk was surrounded by a circular bench. Here, residents were allowed to sit in reverence and silent meditation, holding their pot plants on their knees. Citizens who did this often developed a certain sensitivity. They noticed that strong energy was emanating from the trunk of the tree. They felt it in their backs as a tingling sensation. This was very disturbing, to say the least, as it had been maintained for centuries that the tree was DEAD. It would have amounted to sacrilege to mention this to anyone else, yet the dedicated group of people who noticed this - and who were able to trust each other with their reservations and feelings - met daily at the tree. They nodded to each other and knew intuitively (as the tree had awakened their intuitive abilities) that they were all aware of the same phenomenon - of the secret power of the tree.

These people were – in turn – observed by watching officials. One day, a fence was put up around the tree trunk to prevent people from approaching it closely. The sign said that the fence was necessary "TO BETTER PRESERVE OUR ANCIENT HERITAGE AND IN RECOGNITION OF OUR GUILT AND NEED TO DO PENANCE". Most visitors nodded their heads sadly in agreement. But the group of sensitives had different feelings. They were forced to go "underground" to discuss what was going on. They did this literally, meeting in an old disused cellar. And it was here that they discovered a piece of TREE ROOT emerging from the wall.

After careful examination and experimentation, they pronounced this to be the living root of a living tree. Secretly, they watered the root, which drank it up immediately, as if suffering from a hundred years of thirst. The group continued to feed the root and to encourage the tree to GROW. This in itself would have been considered heresy, as the general rule for pot plants was QUICK GROWTH WILL KILL. Thus "repotting" was against the rules. The idea that a pot plant needed "repotting" was condemned as harmful superstition.

And so, the root grew. When the group visited the garden, they noticed hair cracks in the paving, and they looked at each other with knowing glances. The cracks widened daily, and soon there was another notice which said: "THE GARDEN IS TO BE PRESERVED AS A MONUMENT TO NATURAL BEAUTY, AND CAN THEREFORE NO LONGER BE EXPOSED TO DETRIMENTAL HUMAN CONTACT AND POLLUTION". Most visitors nodded sadly when they saw this sign, and they stood at the locked gates and sent love to the garden.

But still the roots continued to grow. On the streets, cracks started to appear, and road maintenance suddenly became very busy "CORRECTING STRUCTURAL DAMAGE DUE TO DISREPAIR". But this was so widespread that it was impossible to hide or suppress any longer. People wandering through the streets were astonished to find plants and bushes suddenly sprouting through the pavement. This was truly wondrous for those who stopped long enough to feel the beautiful uplifting energy which emanated from the plants. Others rushed away in fright, for this was an impossible phenomenon which did not fit into their worldview. Officials attempted to eliminate the bushes during the darkness of night, but with time, they were observed by the inhabitants, some of whom broke down to see such beauty being destroyed. They could not understand why officials were desecrating the nature which they had so long been protecting, or so they said.

Chaos ensued. The roots were now fully visible and growing at a tremendous rate, especially as the group of sensitives was now openly encouraging the inhabitants to provide them with water, and the response grew by the hour. Buildings were starting to collapse. Some rejoiced in this fantastic development which showed them that nature was truly ALIVE IN ALL ITS GLORY, AND OTHERS LAMENTED THE DESTRUCTION OF THEIR HOMES. THEY CURSED THE ROOTS AND HACKED THEM OFF WHEREVER THEY COULD. BUT THERE WAS NO POINT IN THIS, AS THE GROWTH MOMENTUM WAS SO GREAT. ONE ROOT CUT OFF WAS REPLACED BY SEVEN.

IN THE END, THE VERY ROOF OVER THEIR HEADS BEGAN TO CRACK. When they noticed this, crowds of citizens stormed the gates of their huge, roofed compound, overthrowing the guards who kept watch, and burst beyond the perimeters of their known world, expecting to be met by poisoned air and bare, blackened countryside.

But instead of this, the people discovered lush, abundant fields, and as they looked back at their former grey concrete home, they saw the huge tree at its centre. It was very much alive, and its enormous green crown stretched high into the sky. It was then that the people realised that they had been SLAVES FOR CENTURIES, LIVING A LIE, SUBDUED BY FALSELY ACCREDITED GUILT, ALLOWING THEIR RULERS TO LIVE IN PARADISE AND ABUNDANCE, WHILE THEY THEMSELVES HAD LIVED IN POVERTY WITHIN THE WALLS OF THEIR PRISON.

THE HALL OF TRUTH

A long queue of people stood waiting in front of a simple door. They were all very tense as they had no idea what was awaiting them, but they knew it would be a monumental learning experience. One by one, they were ushered in.

As one woman went through the door, she found herself at the entrance to a huge hall, full of people. As she walked in, all eyes turned towards her. Nothing was said. She felt a rush of great apprehension because she recognised EVERY SINGLE PERSON IN THE ROOM. They had all touched her life at some time in the past, but this was not the focus now. The reason for seeing them now was experiencing HOW SHE HAD TOUCHED THEM.

The woman moved very slowly along a long, central, red carpet. As she did so, she realised that this was THE HALL OF TRUTH WHERE EVERYTHING IS REVEALED. It was not possible for her to overlook someone, to avoid someone, or to invent some excuse to look in the opposite direction. She was forced to LOOK EVERYONE IN THE EYE. And as she did so, everyone responded truthfully. If the woman had treated them well, they smiled. If she had ignored them or treated them disrespectfully, they glared. If she had actively degraded them, they stared malevolently. If she had loved them, they fell upon her in embrace.

At the end of the red carpet was a chair where the Creator sat. She threw herself at his feet, but he bade her to rise saying MY CHILD: I HAVE SEEN AND FELT ALL THE FEELINGS YOU HAVE CREATED IN OTHERS, INCLUDING IN YOURSELF. YOUR RELATIONSHIPS WITH OTHERS ARE MERELY A REFLECTION OF YOUR RELATIONSHIP WITH ME, AS I AM INSEPARABLE FROM YOU, AND I AM INSEPARABLE FROM THEM. PROCEED WITH THIS KNOWLEDGE INTO THE NEW WORLD.

Then the woman was shown out at the back of the hall, and the man at the head of the queue outside was ushered in to take his turn at walking the hall of truth.

THE GOLDEN THREADS

Dark clouds filled the sky all over the earth. Earth's inhabitants went about their usual business in a fairly resigned sort of way. Suddenly golden threads descended from the sky, and everyone who noticed them and touched them were filled with awe, as they came to the RECOGNITION that there were many exciting things of which they were unaware.

Then thousands upon thousands of purple flowers fell through the clouds onto the ground, falling at the feet of the astonished onlookers. Those who noticed the flowers came to the RECOGNITION that whoever was throwing the flowers had the same connection with nature as themselves, and that "nature" could hardly be a phenomenon restricted to this planet alone, but common to a great number of evolving planets. These people felt uplifted and reassured because they now knew they were not alone in the universe.

Then thousands upon thousands of sea-shells descended from the sky. This really confused these inhabitants. They now knew that those above had an affinity with nature, but they usually regarded the sea as a mass of water below, not above. Those who thought about this carefully came to the conclusion that EVERYTHING MIGHT BE THE OTHER WAY AROUND. While this was a disconcerting thought initially, it was also exciting to think that everything might actually be quite different.

Then a hailstorm of small golden balls occurred, but miraculously they did not hit the populace but landed on the ground. As they were extremely hard, made out of a transparent material never seen before, they were picked up and marvelled at. The children were delighted because the balls also bounced, and they began to play with them. Others, very busy with their own routines, did not notice the playing children at all. Those who contemplated this wonder came to the RECOGNITION that those above were technologically much more advanced, and also more spiritually advanced. They showed love instead of hate: they had sent golden balls to play with instead of bullets to kill.

THE DUCKLINGS' JOURNEY

Three very small, yellow ducklings were struggling to swim. Usually, when they became disconcerted or lacking in strength, they would hop onto their mother's back for a rest, but this time, the mother duck was nowhere to be seen. Suddenly, they felt something move below them in the water, and the ducklings were carried along and able to rest, no longer needing to swim. The surface they stood on was not warm and fluffy, like their mother, but it was supportive nevertheless, and so the ducklings travelled effortlessly down the river on the back of an unknown and unseen entity.

As they did so, people began to gather on the shores of the river, watching the ducklings miraculously standing on the water, or so it seemed. They cheered and waved but stayed on the side-lines, not daring to take the plunge. The ducklings basked in their admiration and applause. In the beginning, the ducklings were amazed at this attention, but as they grew into ducks, they came to consider this as normal, expecting crowded banks and enthusiastic cries whenever they made a public appearance.

As the river expanded in width and the banks retreated, the ducks automatically quashed any feelings of unease, propped up by their convictions of self-importance. When they realised that they were approaching the open sea and rougher waves, they became afraid, but swim they could not because they had missed their chance to learn, preferring to stay on the ever-supportive back of the entity carrying them. As always, they relied on their unknown supporter, even more so as they could no longer communicate with their fans on the shore.

It was then, as the waves tossed and turned them, that they saw patches of skin revealed under their feet, and they realised that all this time, they had been in dire danger, riding on the back of a crocodile. And almost at the same moment, they realised that not only one crocodile was making for the open seas, but thousands of crocodiles emerging from the mouths of many rivers, each one carrying ducks on their backs.

The crocodiles all converged, drawn as if by magnetism, to a whirlpool of incomparable depth and strength. No-one could withstand this pull. The crocodiles and their passengers dived into this hole which turned into a black watery tunnel. At the end of the tunnel was an intense light, and on reaching this, the crocodiles disintegrated.

Some of the ducks disintegrated too, yet those who were more kind-hearted were born again inside an egg. The light inside the egg was rosy, indicative of the bright light outside, promising joy, renewal and rebirth, providing that the duck inside could respond to the hope that its experience outside the egg would be beneficial and enrichening. If so, the duckling would be encouraged to peck its way out.

Those celestial beings who had allowed the ducks to reincarnate, sat and watched. They asked themselves whether they would stay in their cosy shell, comforted by the pink light, or whether they would cast the shell aside to step into a new dimension, into more light and clarity, to view limitless horizons.

The celestial beings also wondered whether any of the players would act differently this time around.

Would the little ducklings now notice if they left the banks of their sanity? Would they realise if a crocodile took away their independence? Would they recognize any secret supporters? Would the onlookers on the banks who - realizing that the ducklings were sailing on a crocodile's back - plunge in to save the ducklings? Or would the onlookers again be deceived and simply applaud unseen horrors?

The celestial advisors sighed because although they loved the little ducklings, they knew that they were not allowed to interfere. The ducklings would have to make their own choices and bear the consequences.

CHAPTER 3

PARABLES
WHICH CLARIFY
OUR CHOICES

THE EMERGENCY BRAKE

A very fast train with bullet-proof windows was travelling to a part of the world where the countryside was still beautiful and unblemished. In this place, it was still possible to make a new start, build healthy communities and live off the land. The people on the train had packed all their valuables, and everything necessary for building and maintaining new houses. A great amount of rice and other dried food was also being transported by the train for their use. There were no planned stops on the way to their destination.

The passengers sat silently, full of apprehension. They were happy to be leaving chaos behind, but they could still see it through the window panes. One passenger was in a great state of agitation and INNER CONFLICT. Her compassion for those she was leaving behind grew with every starving child which stretched its arms towards the passing train. It grew with every hovel and every sign of destruction visible from her seat in the clean, comfortable compartment.

In the end, she could bear it no longer. She stood up and gave a speech to all the occupants of the train saying "FELLOW TRAVELLERS: OUR JOURNEY AND OUR INTENT IS NOT MORALLY CORRECT. LOOK UPON THE MISERY AND BONDAGE OF OUR BROTHERS AND SISTERS ON THESE DESOLATE PLAINS, AND OPEN YOUR HEARTS. WE WILL NOT FLOURISH IN OUR SMALL, NEW, PERFECT ENCLAVE, SURROUNDED BY BARBED WIRE, IF WE CANNOT FEEL COMPASSION. WE WILL ATTACK EACH OTHER AND WE WILL BE ATTACKED AND DESPISED BY THE ENVIOUS AND DESPERATE. WE MUST CHANGE, OR PERISH. I AM GOING TO PULL THE EMERGENCY BRAKE AND WE WILL SETTLE RIGHT HERE, AND SHARE ALL."

The other passengers were aghast, but they realised the truth of her words, and so they filed out of the train awkwardly, attempting to speak in friendly tones to the hostile faces which greeted them. When they opened the food carriages and began to distribute the rice, the starved people broke down crying, saying that gods had come to save them. The passengers were truly shocked to see their emaciated bodies and dreadful conditions at such close quarters, and they were humbled to be seen as generous donors. They were also overwhelmed by the gratitude and love shown to them – something which they had never before encountered. They threw all their old ideas and fears away, and started to re-pair and build houses. In fact, they used up everything the train was transporting and which had been intended only for them-selves. Thus, they created the community of which they had dreamed, without completing their long journey to the other side of the world.

THE CYCLE OF DEATH

An elaborate funeral service was taking place in a large church. It involved much pomp and expense, and the clergymen leading the service seemed to be secretly laughing at the gullibility and the grief of the mourners, but their faces were serious. They showed concern, but actually this was just a mask.

A long-established tradition of burying corpses meant that the small graveyard was already crammed with tombstones of all shapes and sizes. There was NO ROOM FOR ANY MORE. Again, the clergymen in charge were fully aware of the principle of reincarnation, and knew that the soul continued its journey in another realm, but they encouraged suppression of this knowledge. They continued conducting rituals and rites to instil the population with fear and helplessness. It was a method of control and of earning money, as the coffins were very ornate and expensive. And an ornate plan accompanied their making. As there was no more room in the graveyard, it was suggested that coffins be floated downriver to another site. Boats for accompanying relatives were also provided. Those who were very upset did not notice that the accompanying boats were all roped to the coffin itself. Others wondered mildly what was going on, but most just accepted that this was some sort of tradition.

It was a dark night and very difficult to see ahead in the inky waters. The only assistance came from the light of a bright moon. Passengers who were more aware noticed that the reflection of the moon stopped abruptly a short way ahead. Sensing that something was very, very wrong, and disconcerted by the increasingly loud sound of rushing water, they cut the ropes tying them to the coffin and struggled to the banks of the river.

Those who sat humbly in the remaining boats, with eyes closed, fell together with the coffin over a huge waterfall, where they all perished on impact in the water below. Slaves and minions of the clergymen were waiting on the shore to collect the broken corpses, so that they too could go through the church service and burial process. And so, the system continued – a vicious circle – with only a few people knowing or suspecting the truth of what was going on.

From that day on, the survivors lived their lives to the full, intensely aware of everything around them, knowing that their choices and behaviour would determine how long destructive circuits of manipulation and exploitation would continue. They knew that they were beacons of light for future generations. Even when they were older, they continued to be beacons of light, for they knew that every word and thought would contribute to their next lives, far beyond the perimeters of their present earthly existence.

ANOTHER WAY

A man in full battle dress, including armour and a protective helmet, was wielding his battle-axe at a stone wall which was BLOCKING HIS PATH. He had an array of weapons at his disposal, and he picked them up one by one to see which would be most effective in destroying the wall. He did this with great courage and determination, feeling proud of his strength, which was obvious for all to see.

A woman in white stood behind him. Inwardly, she was appalled at the violence of his behaviour and language. She waited until the soldier had truly exhausted himself and sat down for a rest. Then she approached him and said DEAR SIR, MAY I SHOW YOU ANOTHER WAY? The man was so astonished that he allowed her to lead him by the hand. After walking a very short distance, they came to some steps which led to the top of the wall. The man could not understand why he had not seen them before. He followed the woman up the steps, on which the words LOVE, COMPASSION and UNDERSTANDING were engraved in large letters.

When they had reached the top of the wall, the man and woman jumped down onto the other side. Here, the man discovered that there were more soldiers, just like himself, trying to hammer down the wall in front of them. He took off all his armour and left it in a pile on the ground. Then he waited till one of the soldiers was completely exhausted before he approached him saying DEAR SIR, MAY I SHOW YOU ANOTHER WAY? And then he showed this soldier the alternative route.

And so, each person who was shown the alternative route laid down his arms and initiated others, showing them the alternative route in their turn. This chain reaction continued UNTIL THE WHOLE WORLD WAS DISARMED AND LIVING IN PEACE.

CHAPTER 4

PARABLES
WHICH STRENGTHEN
OUR SOVEREIGNTY

THE SLAVES THAT WERE NOT

This is the tale of the slaves that were not. They lived in an enormous field, which stretched as far as the eye could see. It was divided into two by a brick wall, about 80 cm high.

On one side of this wall, lines of people on their hands and knees shuffled forward in slow motion. They moved their hands and feet but they never moved their heads. The only view they had was of the feet and the behind of the person in front of them.

They were connected to each other by chains which linked the feet of one person to the hands of the next. But the chains were not actually chains at all: they were thin pieces of thread which could have been snapped very easily.

On the other side of the wall, a similar endless crowd of kneeling people were moving in the opposite direction, completely unaware of the other crowd on the other side of the wall. All were dressed in grey. All had ashen, expressionless faces. Their forward movement was slow, although continuous.

Suddenly, one person stopped in fright because there was an unexplainable patch of light near him. Because he had come to a standstill, the whole line of people following him bumped into the next, and hurt their heads. Some of them started to cry. Others noticed that there was a wall to one side of them.

One man decided that because his path was now blocked, he would try and get up onto the wall instead. In his state of great weakness, this was an untold feat of strength. And so there he sat, on the wall - the only upright person among thousands of kneeling prisoners. This, in turn, cast a shadow over others. One by one, as in a domino effect, people noticed the shadow and started to sit up, looking around in astonishment.

The man on the wall was most astonished of all, for he now saw what was happening on the other side of the wall; it was a mirror image of his own, except that the prisoners had been moving in the opposite direction. The only thing which had kept him moving forward had been the vague idea that - at some stage - he would find a land of "milk and honey" at the end of the wall. At that moment, he realized that he had been GREATLY DECEIVED.

Now, others were managing to stand up, and they were amazed to discover that it was so easy to dispose of their "chains". They wondered why on earth they had not done this before. They wondered what direction they had been going in, and why they had not questioned it. They experimented with their arms and legs, stretching them as if coming out of a long sleep.

And all this time, the patch of light shone strongly on the ground and caused great consternation.

When the people had become a little more used to their own freedom, and when they no longer followed each other about, many lights descended all at once from the heavens, and the people fell down again in fright, screaming "angels have come".

"Indeed, we have", said the angels, and they took the bewildered people by the hand and showed them everything they had been missing - and everything which had been going on - while they were obediently crawling behind each other.

IF OUR EYES ARE OPEN

A number of ice-skaters stood on a frozen river with their eyes closed. They had been told they would be taken on a long exciting journey. The leader asked them to get in line and hold onto each other's shoulders. He positioned himself at the front and guided them across the ice. He was the only one who had his eyes open. He shouted LEFT and RIGHT so that their steps on the ice were perfectly synchronised, and in this way, they got up quite some speed and moved forward rapidly.

The skaters were in good spirits, believing they were on their way to an unknown, remote and possibly exotic destination, and they trusted their leader to get them there safely. At regular intervals, they shouted out I AM HAVING A GREAT TIME or ISN'T THIS FUN or WE ARE DOING THE RIGHT THING or SO GLAD WE ARE DOING THIS TOGETHER.

After many hours of travelling in this way, their leader suddenly stopped saying WELL, THIS MAY NOT BE WHAT YOU EXPECTED, BUT WE HAVE TO STOP HERE. When the skaters opened their eyes, they discovered that they were at EXACTLY AT THE SAME PLACE AS BEFORE - THEIR ORIGINAL POINT OF DEPARTURE.

They sat on the riverbanks in complete shock. What they remembered as never-ending stretches of ice was actually a small icy patch. Two large ships were breaking up the edges of the small icy patch. They were followed by smaller boats with flags flying and music blaring. The boats all wanted the ice to be removed as quickly as possible so that they could continue up or down river to their destinations.

The memory of the skaters was actually intact, but their perception of the journey was erroneous. What had happened was this: the leader had led them cheerfully onwards, down the frozen river. Ever so often there were holes in the ice, indicating that the cold weather was coming to an end, and that the ice was gradually melting. The leader decided to continue the journey, however, carefully manoeuvring the line of skaters behind him so that they avoided the holes. The skaters merely sensed a slight change in direction, and so they thought they were turning a gentle corner.

As the holes became more and more frequent, the leader realised that he would have to turn his group back, still avoiding the ever-increasing numbers of holes. Again, his followers had no idea that they were in danger, or that they had completely changed direction. In the end, only one small stretch of river was still frozen and "safe", and the leader circled round and round this patch endlessly until he saw the icebreakers appear at either side. At this point, the leader said WE HAVE TO STOP HERE.

Unaware of these intermittent stages, the skaters were completely confused. With time, the feeling of helplessness receded as they "filled in the blanks". They decided that they would behave differently in future: they would keep their eyes open and FOLLOW THEMSELVES.

THE BROKEN PROCESSION

In a country far away, there were daily processions through the streets. They were headed by horses under very strict control, walking two by two, mounted by officials in order of rank, with the most important officials leading the procession. They wore crowns, top hats, uniforms or medals which gave them an aura of authority. These were the "kings and queens" who made the decisions. The rest were followers rather than leaders, and wore no distinctive markings at all.

The kings and queens rode very regally with their heads high, aware of the impression they made on the passers-by. They rode continuously, basking in the admiration of the populace, and the villagers turned out regularly without fail to applaud them.

Although most of the followers followed blindly, others were aware of the great rigidity of the processions - the route was always the same, and the pecking order was always the same. The horses and their riders were never allowed to move to another position or look behind them. Those at the very end of the procession were so far behind that they had never actually seen the king and queen leading it, and they became very dissatisfied and restless. They were always straining forward, eager for new experiences and chances, but this was not possible. Neither was it possible to stop and have a rest, or to separate oneself in any way from the other riders.

In the end, the very last rider was so frustrated that he decided to do something which he knew was punishable by death. He turned around and looked behind him. What he saw instilled him with great fear: it was the king and queen at the head of the procession. Their faces were distorted with rage, but despite his desperate act, the last rider felt strangely liberated, as if he had broken an enchantment lasting many centuries. At this very moment, everyone in the procession REALISED THAT THEY HAD BEEN RIDING A MERRY-GO-ROUND.

Some did not want to acknowledge this. They felt that their world was falling apart, and they got off their horses and ran away screaming. They had lost their central pivot, their stability, their point of reference. Others closed their eyes and pretended that everything was alright. Yet others, who were more adventurous, urged their horses to move away, but the leading king and queen simply sat on their horses and tried to carry on as usual, trying to hide their great dismay that their procession was now decimated.

Many of their followers had now deflected. Instead of applause, they now earned the jeers of the villagers. In the end, the remaining group of leaders and the main king and queen were forced to leave. They realised that they had taken part in a gross façade - a play with little meaning. They had controlled others and, like puppets, they had also been controlled.

The horses felt a great sense of freedom and tossed everyone off their backs. They galloped away like the wind, cleansing everything which came into their path. The kings and queens lay there helplessly. Because they had been riding for so long, they had LOST THE ABILITY TO WALK.

Some of the village folk refused to help them, jaunting them about their high and mighty ways and rejoicing in their downfall. They had no sympathy at all. Others, though not impressed by the previous behaviour of the kings and queens, decided to show compassion and mercy. This help was rebuked by all those with hearts of stone, and accepted by those who exercised humility and were able to appreciate the kindness of their former minions. The latter started to interact with the villagers and to show gratitude. Although offers of help were repeatedly made to the remaining few who lay on the ground, they were steadfastly refused. Gradually, the village people gave up, with sadness in their hearts, and left them to fend for themselves.

The villagers now focussed on preparations for a village festival of music and dance. This took place in the evening in a lighted market place. The helpless kings and queens were left unattended in the shadows. They had been given up for good. As their bodies crumpled, their souls emerged and were immediately escorted away by angels of justice. Those who survived gathered to dance with the rest of the village community, to celebrate the beginning of a NEW AGE.

TRANSFORMATION IN THE WHITE CATHEDRAL

Once there was a man who always dressed in white. Through this, he demonstrated his intent to become a shining light in the face of darkness, yet others did not seem to be interested in changing the world for the better.

To invite others to share his cause, he drew a large figure of eight on the ground and sat inside one loop. He gestured to passers-by, knowing that they all had great potential, and invited them to sit in the loop opposite him. He addressed them politely with a few well-chosen words, but did not allow them to enter his own loop.

The first woman sat opposite him, crying and asking for help, but as soon as he had comforted her with soothing words, she stopped and regarded him critically. She became melodramatic, thrashing around and making demands, but he calmly held his ground. Sometimes she stopped shouting to check his reaction, but he remained calm. In the end, she turned round stubbornly and refused contact. Communication ended.

The second person to enter the opposite loop was shy. This woman sat down and started to write, with her body at an angle to the man in white. She was aware of his presence, but did not look up or acknowledge him. She kept repeating to herself: "I am important, I am writing something important, I must not become distracted again, I will do what I want. I must fulfil myself. All else is secondary." Communication never even started.

The third woman who entered the opposite loop never kept still. She bounced in and out of the circle, sometimes completely disappearing, sometimes appearing very close to the man in white. She smiled and talked a lot. She was carefree and seemingly tolerant of other approaches to life, but always confident that she was right. She listened and smiled but went her own way. Communication ended. The man in white heaved a heavy sigh and decided that his method was not working, so he stepped out of the figure of eight and went on his way.

As he walked on, his path was littered with wooden boxes, heaped with soil. He was already familiar with these. They each contained a living person. Their skin was completely white because they had not seen sunlight for a long time. Previous attempts to "free" or "wake up" such persons - by lifting up the box lid for a fragment of a second - had always been thwarted by fear.

The people inside the boxes were used to these brief intrusions and always pulled the lid down again immediately with a bang. However hard one knocked, they would not come out. Many months ago, the man in white had given up hope of freeing them, and had given the order to stop knocking, and to cover the boxes with soil.

However, one imprisoned person noticed that no one had tried to open their box for a long time, and so he began to wonder what was going on. Very carefully, he tried to push up the lid themselves. This time, the lid did not move because of the soil on top.

It was then that the person realised that he had let himself be buried alive, and he started to scream. And as soon as one person in a box started to scream, many people in many boxes started to scream.

At this point, the man in white was joined by many companions. They all carried shovels in their hands, ready to free those who no longer wished to imprison themselves. When the soil was removed, many persons of great potential stepped out into the light, stumbling blindly, shattered by the knowledge that they had spent most of their lives in darkness.

A group of these long-time "prisoners" surrounded the man in white and put him on a pedestal. They wanted to sit at his feet and listen to his words in awe, but the man in white did not allow it. He asked them to stand up and speak their truth one by one.

Then they followed him dutifully in a long line into a huge white cathedral. There were no ornate decorations, not even an altar. The man in white stood where the altar should have been and said I AM A PART OF DIVINITY. When he asked everyone else to go up and do the same, they cowered in fright and pleaded unworthiness. Eventually, amid much emotion, they obeyed.

When this ritual was over, everyone held hands to form a circle, and a tiny shoot of green appeared through a crack in the floor. This grew into a beautiful bush with large white flowers, symbolising that there may be many individuals, but they all spring from the same Divine Source. This Source knows that HOWEVER LONG THEY HAVE LIVED IN DARKNESS, SEEDS ALL HAVE THE POTENTIAL TO DEVELOP INTO A HEALTHY, VIBRANT BLOSSOM.

CHAPTER 5

PARABLES WHICH PROVIDE INSIGHTS INTO OUR LIVES

ALL CHANGE AT CENTRAL STATION

THE RED TRAIN is a stream strain, lunging leisurely along the tracks with all the windows open, screeching and letting off steam at intervals. It cannot be overheard or overlooked, as it belches black smoke into the sky. The chatter, laughter, screams and shouts of its passengers, sometimes hanging out of the windows, shatters the silence of the countryside through which it passes. The people inside rarely notice the exquisite meadows and hills outside – though they have ample opportunity – because they are busy consuming sumptuous meals, moving slowly from one carriage to the next to the next social drinks party.

Extreme anger, passion and pain is also experienced in the red train. Passengers experience the whole barometer of strong emotions, followed by long periods of unconsciousness. Most of them are not interested where the train is going, and most would not contemplate disembarking, because they feel they are living life to the full. They feel that this is their right, and that the train is in service to them. Because they never look out of the window, they do not realise that the train is always travelling on a circular track.

THE BLACK AND WHITE TRAIN is a bullet train which glides from A to B, and back again, at incredible speed. The occupants are faceless and nameless. They are stern and polite if spoken to, which is rarely the case, because no-one instigates casual conversation for no apparent reason. Everyone searches out an empty corner, as far away from others as possible, and everyone lowers their eyes to avoid contact.

If they are reproached for not answering a question, they apologise profusely and then return to their laptop, their book, or whatever requires their undivided attention. Most of the passengers cram the time between A and B with premeditated activity which involves only themselves. They continue to shut out what does not concern them at their place of destination, and then again on the commute back home to A. They never get out at the stops in between, indeed, the fewer stops the better, in view of their clear-cut goals.

THE YELLOW TRAIN is a small local train with only two carriages. It is crammed full of children who giggle, cry, play, dream, clap and sing. Some push and shove, others stare out of the window, others wave at the passers-by. The train has a most unusual schedule: in fact, it has no particular schedule at all. If someone on this train is frantically trying to find a timetable or indication of the final destination, they will be disappointed and disconcerted, for this is a train which travels eternally with no fixed agenda.

When the children are bored or tired, or don't know what to do next, they ring the bell and the train stops. The children spill out onto the fields to run, or into the town to explore, or onto the banks of a river to play, or into an orchard to eat, or onto the grass to sleep. They do not worry, as they know the train is also waiting to take them on the next stage of their journey, wherever that may be, whenever they feel ready and refreshed.

THE BLUE TRAIN is not a train in the usual sense. It has no carriages at all. It is all one carriage without walls of separation. In fact, the front of the train is usually - but not always - welded to the back of the train, and it is possible to pass through a door which connects the two. The track is therefore necessarily circular. The blue train is extremely long, as long as a life-time, and when passengers have walked through the whole length of the train, encountering people and situations on the way, they finally reach this door. The sight of this sudden barrier instils great fear in those passengers with short memories, but those who remember going through the door the last time know that it leads to new and exciting experiences.

In a way, this train is also a combination of all the other trains, as it has a plan, but also makes unscheduled stops. The passengers can decide themselves whether they wish to take time out, or continue their passage towards the door. This train is different in that the staff check the passengers periodically, assessing their situations, providing sustenance and inspiration as necessary, providing that the passengers are willing to listen and accept. The staff keep an eye on the passengers, even if they do not notice. No one – even if they throw themselves out of a window - escapes attention and gets lost forever. Time, on this train, is insignificant. Everyone moves at their own pace, though if anyone gets "stuck", the staff is always on hand to offer help.

While all trains travel in their own way, their tracks all pass through the same CENTRAL STATION. At the end of an era, everyone is forced to disembark at Central Station, even if they decide to continue on the same train moments later. In this TIME OF ALL CHANGE, each passenger will be required to revise their journey so far, and to select a destination which is more in keeping with their divine learning schedule.

WHAT WE DO IN OUR LIVES

The sky had turned a strange, pale yellow, and the wind blew rubbish and leaves down a long street. The scene looked as if it had come straight out of an old movie. People wore shabby, old-fashioned clothes. They shuffled around, waiting in a very long queue. Nobody said much, mostly out of fear, as no one who entered the long, dark building ever came out again. Yet some people were waiting patiently and smiling graciously neverthe-less, trying to put the others at ease.

The long building was actually a courthouse. Each person entered to find themselves on a large platform in front of many spectators. Three people were officiating. They smiled, and then one of them said "Welcome. This is very important. You can see that we have a lot of work to do, and that the situation is very grave, so we will be brief. Please give a summary of your life in one sentence. What did you do?"

One after another, people stepped onto the platform and answered this question. A mother wept saying "I looked after my child". A man shouted "That has nothing to do with you". Another woman whispered "How could all this have happened?" A man hung his head saying "I just carried on". Another protested "I enjoyed myself and I regret nothing". A woman said "I tried to warn them", and a man said "I trusted my intuition". Others announced proudly "I worked" or "I was successful" or "I will fight to the end!". Yet others complained "Everyone else behaved dreadfully" or "I was a failure" or "Nothing went well" or "I suffered".

Some people said nothing at all. Others simply smiled and bowed, and this was an indication that they knew they had accomplished their life's goal, and that they wished to move on. The three dignitaries always smiled and gave the same response: "Yes, we understand. Thank you", and then the people were dismissed and shown out of the door.

Stepping out of this door of the judicial building was like moving from a black and white film into glorious colour. Each person was greeted and supervised by an angelic being. Together, they sat down in beautiful gardens and talked about all aspects of their lives - how they had progressed, where obstacles had prevented progression, and what was the next best suitable step. All this was conducted with infinite understanding and compassion, so that each person was able to deal with the experience in the best possible way.

Those who were still unable to talk, repressing anger and sorrow, were led gently away by their supervisors to a place which was more private and suitable for their learning process.

THE RIDER'S DISCOVERY

A valley lay between two very tall mountains. On the valley floor was a forest of trees and shrubs, but most of them had a withered, stunted appearance. This was due to a very strong, relentless wind which descended from the top of the mountain on the right and from the mountain on the left. Only the sturdiest of plants were able to withstand this simultaneous attack from both sides. There were hardly any new seedlings because they were periodically forced to the ground.

A horse-rider arrived in the forest one day and was astounded to see the damaged condition of the vegetation. He stayed there for a while to observe what was going on, and he noticed that the destructive winds descended in a very regular way from both mountain tops, so he decided to climb them both.

At the top of the mountain on the right, he discovered a very dedicated team of people activating an enormous pair of bellows. They worked in shifts so that wind was continually pumped into the valley. The rider asked why: WE LOVE NATURE MORE THAN ANYTHING ELSE they replied. OUR LEADERS HAVE TOLD US THAT THE PLANTS NEED WIND SO THAT THEIR SEEDS ARE WELL SCATTERED.

At the top of the mountain on the left, the rider found another very dedicated team of workers, also working in shifts to keep a similar pair of bellows providing wind for the valley. Again, the rider asked why: WE LOVE NATURE MORE THAN ANYTHING ELSE they replied. OUR LEADERS HAVE TOLD US THAT WIND IS NEEDED CONSTANTLY SO THAT THE OLD LEAVES WILL DROP AND MAKE WAY FOR THE NEW.

On hearing this, the rider invited both groups down into the forest to see what was going on. Some refused to do this, as their loyalty to the cause prevented them from leaving their posts. Those who sensed the rider's great distress decided to follow him down the mountain. When they learnt about the negative effect of the constant wind from both directions on their beloved trees, they collapsed and cried, knowing that their lack of curiosity and blind allegiance had contributed to this destruction.

THE SEED'S JOURNEY

Imagine you are curled up like an embryo inside a nut with a very hard casing. You understand that GROWING is preceded by a period of abstinence, stillness or restriction FROM WHICH YOU CAN GROW. Yet you also harbour a feeling of limitless expansion; you know you are ONE with all, feeling the hard perimeters of the nut on every surface of your body.

There is an enormous feeling of security in that tightness and darkness as a seed. You know that someone – the CREATOR OF THE UNIVERSE - is covering your back always.

Understand that the next step towards optimal growth is your DECISION to birth yourself, separating yourself temporarily from the ONE. You start to move. You arouse yourself from sleep and are overcome with CURIOSITY. When you knock against the familiar wall of the nut casing, it sounds hollow, so you know without a doubt that there is something BEYOND it. Your extreme DETERMINATION to find that "something" impels you to push relentlessly until the seedling finally cracks its shell and pokes its tender green head into the soil.

Now you are in a completely different environment. Every pore is clogged with soil. You rely on instinct to find your way, stretching your head upwards because the ground above you feels warmer.

COURAGE is needed to leave your old surroundings in search of the new. The desire to grow upwards comes from somewhere deep within: you grow in alignment with a divine blueprint which you do not yet understand in full, but which you learn to trust.

All this brings you towards the surface of the soil where you suddenly burst into the sunlight. You are overcome with ecstasy at this unknown brightness, warmth and expanse which nurtures you, together with the rain. You accept these gifts fully and gratefully, growing rapidly.

You wonder if you will eventually be able to touch the sky. But somehow, the idea of eternal self-perpetuation and growth in one direction only is not appealing, so you begin to spread your branches sideways also.

Thus, you can survey what is happening on the ground. Small children play beneath your branches. When you see that they loved to climb, you grow in a way which enables them to do that, and when you see they are hungry, you are seized with great COMPASSION and you realise that you have the potential to create fruit for their consumption.

When the children see peaches ripening on your branches, it seems like a miracle, and so they are inspired – in their turn - to set out on their life journeys, creating gifts for others through the same chain of growth, through DECISIONS TO SEPARATE FROM THE FAMILIAR, through CURIOSITY, COURAGE, DE-TERMINATION and COMPASSION. Thus, they discover their own unique brand of service to humanity.

EXPLAINING THE SHADOWS AWAY

A man sits in the same office every day, and he knows NOTHING ELSE. His office building is surrounded by other buildings, so he never sees a horizon. As he carries out his daily work, writing notes diligently, he notices that the colour of the paper changes from grey to white, and then to grey again.

He explains this to himself in various ways. Sometimes he says MY EYES ARE WEARY in the morning and in the evening, and therefore the paper is clearer in the middle of the day. Or he says: less electricity is used in the mornings and evenings, and so there is more power in the lamps at midday. And on others days, the man simply does not think at all – he just puts it down to something INEXPLICABLE.

One day, a woman enters the man's office, smiles and says LET'S GO OUTSIDE! The man has no conception of what "out-side" means, and he is so perplexed that he lets himself be led by the hand. She guides him up many flights of steps to the roof of the building. Here, for the first time in his life, he feels the fresh air on his skin, and for the first time, he sees THE SUN RISING AND SETTING. "The sun is the reason for the change in colour" he realises. This puts all his previous experiences in a completely new light, showing him very clearly HOW LIMITED IS HIS TRAIN OF THOUGHT.

And the woman says the following to him, and to everyone she meets: ALWAYS BE READY FOR THE GREAT REWIRING, THIS GREAT REFRAMING OF YOURSELF WITHIN THE NET-WORK OF THE MAJESTIC DIVINE FORCES OF WHICH YOU ARE PART.

CHAPTER 6

PARABLES WHICH INCREASE LOVE AND COMPASSION

WHEN LOVE TRIUMPHS OVER FEAR

A beautiful tropical island came into view. Small groups of inhabitants dotted the white beaches. They lived in great abundance, with huge expanses of jungle and fruit-bearing trees at their disposal. Nothing disturbed their lives, though they sometimes asked themselves why the waves were sometimes rougher than usual, or encroached more on the land than usual, although the skies were continuously storm free. As a result, a current of unease began to grow.

This unease was exacerbated by boats full of "foreigners", who attempted landings to steal fruit from the abundant orange groves. When they appeared on the horizon, the inhabitants of orange island shouted GO AND EAT YOUR OWN ORANGES.

As this development became more marked, the inhabitants of remote villages, who would usually never arrange to meet intentionally, felt drawn to discuss what was happening. Meetings were held. Leaders with a passion emerged, pronouncing that something had to be done to stem the rising tides, prevent flooding and stave off invasion. Some of the hardliners began to build a sea wall, yet they were forced to realise that there was no point building a wall in front of their own particular part of land, if nobody else was going to do the same.

Though the hardliners held the other groups in great contempt, they were forced to co-operate with them on a superficial level, so that they could be manipulated into building their own sea walls.

Campaigns to enclose the island ensued, and over the years, the gorgeous beaches and lush undergrowth gave way to concrete fortresses. The orange plantations suffered and diminished until in the very end, only one tree remained, and the old way of life had all but been forgotten in the mists of time. The health of all the islanders had degenerated simultaneously. They lay around lethargically and fearfully within the confines of their castles. The only remaining orange tree was fiercely protected by the regent, and the oranges were reserved for his consumption and that of his close followers only.

Just as everyone was on the point of final demise, they sighted many ships on all horizons. Their instinctive reaction – based on the attempted foreign invasions of the past – was fear, but they were too weak to prepare for battle. They had no option but to wait until these tall strangers dressed in white landed on their shores with their blades held high.

But this expectation was erroneous. The strangers walked slowly, with great care and compassion, investigating all as if taking stock of the situation and assessing what would be the next best step to take in these circumstances. They did not speak; they just looked with great understanding, putting a hand on the shoulders of the inhabitants to calm them if necessary. The villagers realized that these were not enemies at all, as they had thought, but people who sought to unite them and rebuild their society.

THE WALL OF GLASS

A king and queen and their high-ranking followers were riding inside a white carriage gilded with gold. The horses made good progress, and all appeared to be well, despite the grim faces of the peasants which they glimpsed through the windows as they passed. For these "dignitaries" on the inside of the carriage, it seemed as if the sun was shining, but outside the carriage, it looked as if it was raining. The situation outside did not command their attention, however.

Suddenly the horses started to flounder. Instead of the hard road underfoot, they were now struggling through thick piles of moss at the banks of a river. The travellers were jerked out of their complacence. They were astounded because they had no previous recollection of a river at this location. They were force to dismount, and curiosity led them to climb the ridge where the river appeared to have its source. Beyond the ridge, a new horizon greeted and astonished them, for here lay a large lake surrounded by crowds of weeping people. The lake was salty and consisted of tears.

When the weeping people saw the king and queen, the rulers of their "serfdom" and the creators of their misery, their sadness turned to anger and they started to charge towards them. Just before they reached their rulers, however, they smacked into a HUGE TRANSPARENT WALL OF GLASS WHICH KEPT BOTH SIDES SEPARATED.

The rulers saw AT VERY CLOSE HAND the tears and anger on the faces of the multitudes. They recognised their failure to look after their people. And the people saw AT VERY CLOSE HAND the shock, confusion and regret on the faces of their rulers. The people recognised their failure to go into action to defend their rights. No one could actually hear what words were being said on the other side of the glass, but the emotions were very clearly seen and registered.

Without the wall, there would have been immediate violent conflict. The wall allowed everyone to clearly see the consequences of their actions. Both parties were better able to understand each other. When the wall suddenly disappeared, they were able to approach each other with dignity and to search jointly for the best solution for all.

THE SECOND WALL OF GLASS

Two armies were preparing for battle. One army was dressed in white, and the other in black. At the sound of the trumpets, the members of the white army became very excited. They swung up into the saddles of their horses with great joy and anticipation, not harbouring the wish to kill but hoping to persuade the members of the black army to lay down their arms. The army in black saw the trumpet call as an opportunity to descend upon their enemies and deal them a deadly blow. They uttered blood curdling screams as the two armies were about to clash.

But clash they did not, for an almost invisible glass wall sprung up and partitioned the two armies off at the very point where they were supposed to meet. Most of the members of the white army got off their horses and smiled at their "opponents" through the glass, making welcoming gestures. The glass itself emitted a sort of energetic glow, repelling all those who did not harbour good intentions. As a result, some of the white-clad horsemen, who secretly harboured impure thoughts, turned to grey. Those who remained white looked at them sadly and rounded them up, for they were clearly traitors.

On the other side of the wall of glass, the black army was all the more infuriated to see smiling faces. They shouted in anger and attacked the glass, resulting in considerable injury to themselves. Some members of the dark army hesitated, wondering what to do next. They saw the strength of their fellows, yet they saw the futility of their actions. Yet others waited with great anticipation, for they had hearts of white though their clothes were dark.

Suddenly a row of angels appeared between the white army and the glass. They spoke in unison so that everyone could hear. COME TO US, whispered the angels to the "dark brothers". IF YOUR HEART IS WHITE AND FULL OF LOVE, YOU WILL BE

ABLE TO TRAVERSE THE GLASS WALL. BUT IF YOUR HEART IS FULL OF ANGER AND DESTRUCTIVE INTENT, THE POWER OF THE GLASS WILL DESTROY YOU.

The angels were very serious in their address. They indicated that this was the last chance for anyone to save themselves. Those who had been waiting in the background recognised this and, holding all the love that they could muster, they approached the glass partition and walked through it, to be welcomed by the angels on the other side. Now it was clear to all what was happening. A loving heart was needed to cross over to safety. Self-destruction was the alternative. The angels appealed repeatedly until the very last person had made their choice between LOVE AND HATE.

THE BEAR AND THE BOY

A small, shabby, travelling circus in a distant country was setting up camp at a new location. The bear-tamer was training a large, old bear with a stumbling gait and dishevelled fur. To make it "dance" on two legs, the trainer hung a carrot on a string and dangled it in front of the bear's nose. The bear was immediately hypnotised by the carrot and followed it wherever it went, in the hope of getting its next meal. It was only after a long time had passed that the trainer actually allowed the bear to get hold of the carrot. On finding that the carrot did not satisfy his hunger, the bear was extremely disappointed.

In his anger, the bear ran off to the forest where he discovered a boy in a clearing. The frightened boy offered him food, and the bear was now faced with a dilemma. He was so hungry by now that he could have eaten the boy in one bite, which would have been more satisfying than eating the food the boy offered him.

On the other hand, maybe the boy would become his friend, and provide him with food on a regular basis.

The bear decided to graciously accept the food, and he and the boy became the best of friends. The trainer lost his source of income, just as he had lost his kindness toward animals. When he saw the close friendship shared between the bear and the boy, he learnt that he had acted in a reprehensible way, and he asked the bear for forgiveness.

GAIA'S TRANSFORMATION

The earth, known as Gaia, appeared as an old woman wearing shabby, black clothes. She always had her arms outstretched, as if asking for something, and thus she walked haltingly down the busy streets of a large city. She was largely ignored by the smart urbanites who passed her by. They always walked swiftly and turned their heads away, for they did not wish to be distracted from "important business". Others took pity on the old woman and placed a coin or loaves in her outstretched hands, but this did not seem to satisfy her. The pained expression on her face never changed.

As Gaia became more and more crippled, she was no longer able to reach the pedestrian precincts of the inner city, and so she sat forlorn on the outskirts where very few people passed her at all. One day a black limousine slowed down and stopped beside her. The window opened, and someone threw a huge gold coin into her lap. Then the car drove off.

This seemed to be the breaking point for Gaia: she flung the coin high up into the air screaming "I DON'T NEED GOLD: I NEED LOVE!". As she screamed with pain and rage, she transformed herself into a huge, black whirlwind which tracked all over the earth's surface to places where great damage had been done – open mines, polluted rivers, desecrated countryside. When she saw these places, she wept bitterly. Wherever she passed, the whirlwind spilt the ground creating deep fissures and earthquakes to relieve pressure. And Gaia cleansed the ground with rivers of tears.

When all places of destruction and violation had been purged and restored, Gaia was able to rest. She chose a small green hill covered in meadow where she slept for a long time. Like a snake shedding its skin, Gaia's outer mantel dissolved to reveal a beautiful young girl who smiled in her sleep, dreaming of a new world where LOVE IS EVERYWHERE.

THE PREGNANT EARTH GIVES BIRTH TO A NEW AGE

There once was a person called Earth - a huge and highly pregnant woman. She was crying and shaking, and she was desperately in need of comfort, as if she knew that the birth was imminent and that it would be painful, however glorious the outcome. Inside her stomach, rivers of lava were coursing with greater and greater fury. People had bored holes into her skin and had detonated explosives. Poison had been poured into her veins. She was breathing toxic air. She was forced to process dangerous waste. Her treasures had been excavated. Her organs had been ruptured.

Rocking and massaging her was not enough to counteract all this abuse, which had been going on for millennia. She needed spiritual protection and encouragement, so celestial beings appeared and placed amethysts at her feet and surrounded her in a large protective bubble. This helped her to regain her balance and relax.

One of earth's inhabitants, a midwife, felt intuitively that the earth must be going through incredible birthing pains. As the midwife wandered about the countryside, helping pregnant women everywhere, she trod cautiously on earth's "skin", knowing how humanity had exploited and desecrated the ground she walked upon.

"HOW CAN WE MAKE EARTH A SACRED PLACE AGAIN?" asked the midwife as she crossed a beautiful hilly landscape without roads.

One path lead through a forest where the trees had faces and arms, and other "human" features. Here, the midwife heard the answer to her question: YOU CAN MAKE THE EARTH MORE SACRED BY RESPECTING THE TREES AS YOUR LIVING SISTERS AND BROTHERS.

She walked on through the autumn sunshine, treading on many dead leaves with human faces. Here, the midwife heard another answer to her question: YOU CAN MAKE THE EARTH MORE SACRED IF YOU ARE CONSTANTLY AWARE OF THE CYCLES OF RENEWAL.

Then she walked into a field where lots of small children were laughing and playing with baby lambs. Here she heard another answer: YOU CAN MAKE THE EARTH MORE SACRED IF YOU PROTECT THE INNOCENT AND CELEBRATE ALL LIFE.

Then she walked into a village where she greeted the local people, and here she heard the answer: YOU CAN MAKE THE EARTH MORE SACRED IF YOU VALUE EACH ENCOUNTER, AND IF YOU ACT WITH RESPECT AND GRACE TOWARDS EVERYONE YOU MEET.

Then the midwife continued her travels, walking further afar to other countries, and she was greeted by Kings, Queens and dignitaries. There she heard the answer: YOU CAN MAKE THE EARTH MORE SACRED BY DEVELOPING PEACEFUL RELATIONS AND CO-OPERATION WITH OTHER NATIONS.

When she looked upwards towards the sky, she saw many stars and planets, and then she heard the answer: YOU CAN MAKE THE EARTH MORE SACRED IF YOU SUPPORT HER DESIRE TO RECONNECT WITH HER CELESTIAL FAMILY FROM WHOM – OUT OF LOVE FOR HER INHABITANTS – SHE HAS LONG BEEN SEVERED.

Then the midwife climbed to the top of a nearby mountain and stood with arms outstretched. It was here that she received the most important answer of all: YOU CAN MAKE THE EARTH MORE SACRED BY RECOGNISING YOURSELVES AS GODS AND GODDESSES, LIVING UNDER DIVINE GUIDANCE, EMPOWERED WITH THE ABILITY TO CREATE POSITIVE CHANGE THROUGHOUT THE UNIVERSE.

The midwife finally understood that SHE WAS A MAJOR AGENT OF CHANGE. Now, when she walked on earth's lush undergrowth, the cells on the soles of her feet sang songs which vibrated through the ground beneath. Each step was a prayer, a gift given and received - a duet between two surfaces meeting. Her hand embraced branches to become one. Cells greeted one another, exchanging information and transforming as a result of the encounter. The midwife's face bowed to the earth, in mutual respect, each cell whispering love and receiving love's whispers. Her breath met earth's breath – the wind – to sing exquisite harmonies. The scent of earth's coloured petals delighted her senses, and she danced over the grass, blessing it with every step.

The midwife's actions were an inspiration for others, and in the end, everyone offered their love to the earth in this way. At last the ground was free to breathe through every pore, soaking up all light, gratitude and adoration, and thus Earth was inspired to produce abundance for herself and for all grateful inhabitants who granted her peace, recuperation and repose. All this enabled her to give birth to a new age of peace.

CHAPTER 7

PARABLES
WHICH FOSTER
SPIRITUAL VALUES

MONEY TAKES SECOND PLACE

A king was riding a white horse through a forest. He looked tired, as if carrying the weight of the world on his shoulders, so he removed his heavy crown and placed it on the stump of a tree in the middle of a clearing. Full of joy, he made a daisy-chain and put that on his head instead. Feeling light and happy, he galloped off.

The tree stump was the regular meeting place for a group of people who meditated together to seek wisdom. They were astonished to see the crown on the tree stump, but continued to meditate as usual. The message they all internally received was SEEK, BUT DO NOT LOOK FOR REWARD. They were told to leave the crown behind, to go their various ways, and to meet again after a prescribed period of time. Some decided to live simply as hermits in the forest. Others went to help poor neighbouring villages. Yet others became teachers, bakers, musicians, farmers or actors. But one meditator could not forget the glittering crown and, mesmerised by its dazzling gold, decided to begin trading with gold coins. By the end of the given period, he had amassed a fortune, but he was extremely tired and worn.

When the meditators met again in the middle of the forest, they shared their newly gained knowledge, skills and produce. Some sang, some danced, some held speeches, some provided food, and everyone seemed content, except for the gold trader. He had worked so hard to acquire his gold coins that he did not want to give them away. The more he received gifts from his fellows, the more uncomfortable he felt, until in the end, he too began to share his wares. The coins were politely and gratefully received and put away in pockets, but they did not generate the wave of delight and laughter which the trader expected. It was then that he realised that happily shared experiences are worth more than all the gold in the world.

THE MODEL TEACHERS

A group of meditators were sitting in a very large circle at the earth's north pole, but the climate was mild. They were all joined together by streams of energy – a circuit which started from a sphere of light above them. The circuit descended through their bodies to the core of the earth, returning via the same route to connect up with the sphere of light above.

In addition, all the meditators were connected to each other by golden strands, forming an intricate golden network. As the meditators concentrated on sending out love energy, in order to increase the vibrations of their surroundings, the entire flow of the circuit increased and threw off sparks which fell on areas which needed this uplift.

The extraordinary element in this scene was that the ground was completely transparent, as were the hills in the distance. The meditators were sitting on a sea of glass, and when they looked down, they could see bright blazes and flows of lava beneath them, but still they managed to retain their composure. They even felt that they benefitted from this warmth, in fact, they felt INFUSED by light from both above and below.

After a period of intense meditation, the meditators felt intuitively that they should now SPREAD the light which they had absorbed. They were to BE LIGHT and BE TRANSPARENCY. They separated and went their different ways as teachers, entering classrooms far and wide. Thus, the network of golden strands, which was still attached to every person, was vastly stretched, but still remained intact.

As teachers, the meditators taught sorrowful, bewildered and sometimes angry and very disappointed students who were suffering the collapse of a lifetime of convictions, struggling to understand new concepts of life. In the face of this challenge, the teachers strived to always remember their instructions, which were as follows:

ALWAYS DEMONSTRATE IMPECCABLE BEHAVIOUR

ALWAYS REMAIN HONEST AND RECOGNISE YOUR LIMITS

TEACH WHAT YOU KNOW AND ADMIT WHAT YOU DO NOT KNOW. SAY "I AM NOT SURE", if that is the case.

SHUT YOUR EYES BRIEFLY AND GO WITHIN to find answers to difficult questions.

CONVEY THE IMPORTANCE OF HONESTY, CLARITY AND EAGERNESS TO EMBRACE LEARNING PROCESSES.

INTRODUCE HUMOUR AND DEMONSTRATE JOY.

DO NOT INDULGE ANY ONE DIRECTION FOR TOO LONG, AS THIS WILL HINDER PROGRESS.

BE COMPASSIONATE, BUT NOT CONTINUOUSLY. EXCESS COMPASSION WILL SLOW DOWN FORWARD MOTION.

REMEMBER THAT FORWARD MOTION WITHOUT COMPASSION WILL ALIENATE.

PRACTICE, ILLUSTRATE AND BE THE SORT OF PERSON YOU WISH YOUR STUDENTS TO BE.

ALWAYS STRIVE FOR BALANCE.

LIVING IN THE LIGHT

Seagulls started to gather on the shore of a vast ocean. At first, this was no real surprise for the passers-by, but as the flock of birds grew larger and larger, this attracted some attention. After a while, they were joined by other wild animals who streamed towards the beach in their hundreds. All the animals gathered there, facing the waves in anticipation.

The inhabitants were intensely curious also, eager to observe this phenomenon and find out what it meant. They camped out on the beach with the animals who seemed not to notice them much at all.

One morning a golden ship appeared on the horizon, and all the animals were suddenly intensely alert and focused on the distant waves. As the ship approached, the prow was visible – a golden figure of a man with outstretched arms. The people grew very excited and started to make preparations for the dignitaries who - they assumed - were about to land. They ordered a long red carpet, put up luxurious tents and prepared large banquets. After a while, everything was ready, but the ship remained offshore.

For a while, the people waited with breathless anticipation and excitement, but after a few days they gradually started to lose their patience and discuss in small groups. Some mutinied against the others. Some ransacked the food, saying it was not needed after all. Some returned to their own homes. Some took over the tents and gave orders. And all the time, the animals con-tinued their lives on the beach, happily regarding the ship from time to time.

Seeing the ungracious behaviour and impatience of his fellows, one man stood up and declared that WAITING was the wrong attitude and that it might be time to try something different. His audience was startled and did not understand what he meant.

LET US BE LIKE THE ANIMALS, said the man. LET US SIT IN SILENCE WITH OUR HEARTS OPEN AND OUR ARMS OUT-STRETCHED, AND CONNECT WITH THOSE IN THE BOAT.

As everyone was at a bit of a loss, they decided to adopt this unusual idea. The moment they stood in peaceful unison with their faces towards the ocean, willing to submit to whatever might happen next, a sheet of light emerged from the ship and satu-rated them with a wonderful feeling of lightness, exhilaration and gratitude.

It was then that they realised that this light had always been avail-able to them, and that the animals were LIVING IN THIS LIGHT ALL THE TIME.

When everyone had drunk their fill of this light source, the ship turned and slowly headed out to sea.

THE COFFEE THAT CAME JUST AT THE RIGHT TIME

A man entered a café and sat down at a table, desperate for a cup of coffee. He placed his order but had to wait because there were so many customers. The man felt impatience rising inside him.

Not being able to contain himself any longer, he screamed at the waiter at the top of his voice: "WHERE IS MY COFFEE? WHY IS THIS TAKING SUCH A LONG TIME?".

The waiter smiled and produced another menu card. "Perhaps you might like to read this", he suggested. The man was seething with anger but decided to see what the waiter had given him. He was astounded to read the following:

THE COFFEE APPRECIATION MEDITATION

Expressions of gratitude while waiting for a coffee

To all these, my deepest thanks;

To the Earth who grows the coffee beans

To the Earth who nourishes the man who looks after the cow which produces the milk

To the Earth who produces the metal ore beneath her skin

To the Earth who nourishes the person who extracts the molten metal to make the can

To the Earth who allows the extraction of water from her sources

To the Earth who fires the electricity grid which heats the water

To the Earth who feeds the person who attends to the coffee machine

To DIVINE CHANCE which gifts us with the opportunity to discover these interconnections on an eternal voyage of discovery.

On reading this, the man was overcome by a feeling of intense gratitude and a great sense of calm. He started to think about the carpenter who had built the chair he sat on. He felt gratitude for those who kept the tables clean and who disposed of the rubbish. He thought about his past and of all the people who had helped him. He even felt gratitude for those he could not remember, but who may have given him a smile or a word of encouragement as a toddler. He felt gratitude for his parents, for guiding him through his early years. In fact, he felt gratitude for every experience he had ever had, for he had increased in wisdom. Finally, he gave gratitude to the waiter who was making him "wait", and who had granted him this grand opportunity to reflect on the power of gratitude. This reverie continued until it was broken by the words "Here is the coffee you ordered, sir".

CHAPTER 8

PARABLES
WHICH PREPARE US
FOR GREAT CHANGE

THE DOOR

Once upon a time, there was a fairly prosperous country en-closed by a very large wall along its borders. No one knew what lay beyond. At one point, the wall ran up the ridge of a high hill. At the very apex, a huge wooden door was embedded in the wall. Beautifully carved and gilded with gold, it depicted harmonious patterns and scenes of prosperity. Rumours throughout the ages had suggested that this was the GATE TO THE KINGDOM OF HEAVEN.

It was a popular place to visit for those who believed this, and also for those who did not. The believers, dressed in white, often sat on the steps leading to the gate, singing songs or counting holy beads, asking passers-by for food. Others posed in front of the gate for photographs and laughed loudly. Guards were al-ways stationed there on the orders of the king of this nation. These guards were always encouraging people to move on, pushing away those who stood in reverence for too long.

The king himself scorned those who visited the gate and who made it the final destination of their pilgrimage. He told these pil-grims that the KINGDOM OF HEAVEN could be enjoyed here in the cities (not on the top of a hill) where there were all sorts of pastimes and entertainments capable of providing "heaven". He made a public laughing stock of all those people who lingered for the greatest part of their lives near the gate, in the hope that it would one day OPEN.

Over time, the guards stationed at the gate felt that their work there was degrading. They would have preferred active service, rather than warning people continuously that this was simply a historical artefact with no special religious significance. Their dis-satisfaction led to frequent "desertion of duty". They took turns to leave the site and enjoy the "night life" on offer in the city. In the end, none of the soldiers could resist the banquets, the orgies and the drinking contests, and so the door was often left unguarded.

It was on one of these evenings that the door opened, very quietly and almost unperceptively, and a luminous figure emerged and said: IF YOU CARRY LOVE IN YOUR HEART, YOU MAY NOW ENTER THE KINGDOM OF HEAVEN.

Those believers who spent their nights sleeping near the gate were strangely roused by this voice. When they saw the crack of light coming through the open door, and the figure calling to them, they dropped onto their knees in gratitude and moved swiftly towards the gap before the gate closed again. One such believer was a little slow due to a severe limp, and so a small piece of his cloak ripped off and got caught in the gate as it closed.

In the pale morning light, the guards were astonished to find a small patch of dark cloth clamped between the doors. It could not be removed. Some of the guards said it was just a joke, but others knew that this was a sign – however small – of something much greater, and they redoubled their efforts to keep watch over the gate. They stood directly in front of the cloth so that no-one could see it.

When the daily visitors arrived, they noticed a change in the air. There was more tension. The soldiers were on edge. They cursed and shouted much more than usual. They scoured the horizon as if expecting something unusual, and they gave each other meaningful looks.

The visiting believers threw each other searching glances. They became more and more convinced that the gates would open, so they congregated on the hill more and more frequently, quietly encouraging others to do so. But still there were many who condemned the gates and their supposed promise as gross superstition. They quoted examples of many other similar beautiful doors which had absolutely nothing behind them. And they went through the crowds distributing free tickets to shows and banquets in the city.

The soldiers were now on guard around the clock. One night, they heard a small creak, and the gates opened just wide enough to let one person pass. Again, it was the luminous figure who spoke saying OPEN YOUR HEARTS, FOR ALL THOSE WITH OPEN HEARTS MAY ENTER THE KINGDOM OF HEAVEN. When the soldiers attempted to move towards the figure, they found that they were rooted to the spot. The figure said: RELEASE YOUR WEAPONS. PUT YOUR HAND ON YOUR HEART, AND YOU MAY ENTER.

Again, a number of believers were attracted to the light beyond the gate, and they disappeared through the gate. The soldiers did not know what to do. To tell the king would be signing their own death warrant, so they just continued to keep guard. They lined the whole wall with soldiers, so that the gate was barely visible.

One evening, as they surveyed the dying light of day and the dancing lights of the city below, they noticed a large dark wave approaching – like a rolling carpet of cloud, carried forward by the wind in huge loops. This came from all directions. It seemed to be rounding up all inhabitants, bringing them to the gate. Tightly packed crowds of panic-stricken people were now gathered on the hill, anxiously surveying the onslaught of the "storm".

And for the very last time, the gate opened and the luminous figure appeared: he spoke very clearly and quietly, and he was heard by every single person. No one could interrupt him because everyone had been stunned into silence by the approaching wave. The only sound was the voice of the man saying: IF YOU HAVE LOVE IN YOUR HEARTS, STEP FORWARD AND ENTER.

Those who were not capable of doing this remained as paralysed statues in the darkness, and those who felt humility and love walked to the top of the hill. When all these people had passed through the gates, it shut.

The bodies of those who remained outside turned into stone obelisks, as a warning for civilisations to come, while their souls were taken by angels to another place, in order to determine how they might best learn to love.

RECOGNISING THE MUD

In a small medieval town, people wearing bonnets, top hats and long, old-fashioned clothing were bustling about in the streets, busily greeting each other and moving on as quickly as possible to their destinations. They did not linger, and they were always alert, never looking down. They took pride in their connections, wanting to be on good business terms with everyone, and so they kept a sharp lookout for whoever might turn the corner next. They always had a pleasant greeting on their lips, waiting for the next acquaintance to suddenly appear.

When they reached their houses or businesses, the first thing they did was take off their shoes, leaving them outside the door. These shoes were ENCRUSTED WITH MUD, but this mud never reached their owner's feet, because all shoes were positioned at the top of tall stilts. The residents were very accustomed to walking in this cumbersome way. Many did not even ask themselves why this was so. If the residents had looked down onto the streets, they would have seen a river of mud and sewage.

One night, a group of activists decided that it was time to make a move. They felt it was impossible to tolerate the mud any longer, and they knew it had to be removed. In the middle of the night, they ran around the town, gathering up all shoes which were standing outside the doors.

When the residents woke up the next morning, preparing to leave the house as usual, they found that their shoes were gone. Some people said to themselves OH WELL, BUSINESS AS USUAL, and left the house in slippers. They were delighted to be able to walk so fast on the pavements, but they were appalled when they sunk to their knees in grime and sewage when trying to cross a street. It was the first time that they had really been aware of the mud. In the end, everyone was forced to stay at home indefinitely and consider a solution.

THE WHITE SHIP

A very large, white ship was travelling slowly through steep gorges. Despite its size, most people did not see it. They did not dare to venture as far as the precipice, and if they did, they were very perturbed by the sight of the narrow, dangerous path leading down to the river banks. Although it was possible to manage the steep descent, climbing back up was nearly impossible, due to loose stones. Nevertheless, those who heard the ship's horn and felt irresistibly but inexplicably drawn to it, followed intuition and climbed down. The others continued with daily life, hearing the distant horn from time to time, but not paying it much attention.

Those who boarded the ship were welcomed with open arms. The owners had painted the words LOVE, HONESTY, RE-SPECT, GRATITUDE and DIVINE GUIDANCE on the sides of the ship along the water-line. Meditation sessions took place at night on the deck, after which everyone lay down with blankets and watched the stars which glittered, changed colour and sent uplifting energy.

During the day, meetings were held. Some of the travellers on board were capable of leaving their physical bodies behind, and they returned to their home towns to observe what was going on. They investigated how susceptible people were to the higher vibrations of love. They discovered that some were very unhappy, suspecting there was more to life than their daily drudge. The travellers returned to the ship with the advice to continue sounding the horn to alert all those with the courage to leave everything behind and make a change for the better.

The ship continued to sail. Some people on board became impatient. They talked to the captain and told him to sail faster, or to sound the horn louder, or to send more obvious signs out to the people in the towns, but he refused saying that this would have no effect. He would not use force, and he would not use fear to manipulate them. Thus, the ship continued slowly as usual, sounding its horn gently at long intervals.

At the end of a long journey, the ship arrived in a wide estuary, and then it reached the open sea. Here, the nearby communities lived right on the shore. Effortlessly, the travellers stepped off the ship and into crowds of people who had gathered there, wondering where the ship came from. The travellers realised that they had reached their destination, and they immediately set up their teaching mission, instructing their new-found students about ways to change their lives for the better and for the benefit of all.

THE JOURNEY FROM DARK TO LIGHT

A group of people gathered in order to increase earth's vibrational frequency. They sat on a hilltop around a camp fire and simultaneously went into a meditative state, fixing their attention on the flames. The more energy they sent in that direction, the higher the flames grew. Each person sent their own particular energy to the flames which was visible as a single coloured beam of intense light.

After a while, the flames started to crackle loudly and spit baubles into the air. These were multi-coloured, like spherical rainbows, and large birds carried them in their beaks to places on earth where great distress reigned. These were dirty, colourless, depressed places where the inhabitants had lost all hope. Here the birds dropped the baubles. They burst as they hit the ground, releasing beautiful pools of multi-coloured water.

Half of the population in these depressed areas was so suspicious, resigned and entrenched in their own lives and problems that they scarcely raised their head when they saw these pools. They practically ignored them, immediately dismissing them as a trap or a deceptive mirage. But some noticed the pools and – if their courage was great enough – they approached them and tested the water with a finger. The moment they did so, a feeling of lightness and joy spread from their finger, up their arm, and into the rest of their body, and they were infused with a great optimism for the future.

The small children had no inhibitions; they screamed with delight and immediately jumped into the pools, splashing around with delight. This caused yet more multi-coloured baubles to rise into the air, and again the birds arrived to carry these new baubles to yet more depressed and deprived areas on earth.

This process, which had been initiated by the meditators on the hill, continued to spread until the whole surface of the earth was covered in brilliant multi-coloured light. It was unavoidable. It was no longer possible to hide in a dark corner, because dark corners no longer existed. It was no longer possible to retreat from the great wave of optimism, joy and enthusiasm which was being evoked. Those who continued to resist were removed by angels and relocated to places where they could continue to live in the way they personally chose to do so, in a degree of less intense light which was more suitable for their spiritual growth.

THE SHIP THAT NEVER LANDED UNTIL NOW

Two men stood at the helm of a very dark, windowless tanker, deep at sea. Their bodies, but also their minds, were numbed by the constant cold and rain. Their only instructions – to which they strictly adhered out of fear - were to direct the ship towards isolated waters and NEVER LAND. They knew that there was something of extremely high value in the hulk of the ship, but they had no idea what it was. Their voyage had been going on for so long that they had forgotten how many years they had been underway. Their entire passage had been so stormy that they had forgotten what the light of day looked like.

One evening, when the storms were even more intense than usual, and when the sailors were in fear for their very lives, a very bright sword of light appeared and literally cut a hole into the flank of the great ship, striking terror into the hearts of the sailors and nearly blinding them. The hole was shaped like a heart, and as a result, a heart-shaped path of light emitted and pierced the storm clouds, projecting a heart image onto the sky. This emanated from a huge glittering crystal in the innards of the ship.

The sailors asked WHAT IS THIS? And the crystal replied: I AM THE KNOWLEDGE OF THE DIVINE ONE AND ALL, OF WHICH YOU ARE PART. MY LIGHT HAS BEEN CONCEALED BUT CAN NEVER BE OBLITERATED. TAKE HEART, FOR NOW THE DARKNESS WILL DISSIPATE.

People living on a nearby island, who had also lived in dark depression for many years, came out of their hiding places and rejoiced on the beaches, for this was a sign that everything would change. Trembling with fear and joy at the same time, the sailors decide to contravene orders and steer for land. Here, angels appeared and removed the crystal onto land for all to see. The power of the crystal was so great that the whole earth was cleansed, and not even the tiniest cloud remained to sully the brilliant blue sky.

The sailors were so overcome that they fell on their knees to the ground, asking for forgiveness. Gently, the angels raised them up and took them away for further questioning.

THE INEVITABLE HARVEST

Once there was a large orchard. All the apple trees were at varying stages of growth, and of various age, but they were all subject to the same weather and the changing seasons. This meant that the period of growth and the period of harvesting was the same for all trees. The cycle had to be completed before the colder weather appeared, otherwise it would be impossible to gather the fruits due to thick layers of snow. It would also be pointless to harvest decaying, frozen fruits.

In autumn, many farmers gathered to collect the harvest. First, they spotted a diseased tree which looked completely black. Although the fruit it bore looked surprisingly large and luscious, the farmers did not trust this, and they partitioned the black tree off, so that it should not contaminate the others.

Then they attended to the other trees. First, they collected the "windfalls". These fruits had not had the strength to hold their own against the high winds. Then they picked the ripe apples which were at the exact point of maturity for harvesting. They left the small, unripe apples still on the tree, hoping that they would develop quickly before the onset of winter.

Just before the onslaught of colder weather, the farmers knocked down all the remaining apples whether they were ripe or not. All apples were sorted according to size and quality. Some were sold at market, some were made into juice, others were fed to animals.

The luscious large fruits on the black tree were destroyed, as was the tree itself, especially the roots, as they were discovered to be poisonous. Thus was the harvest complete.

NAVIGATING THE MAP IN DIVINE HANDS

A young girl wandered around a huge city looking for somewhere to live. She was new to city life, and she stared at everything with large innocent eyes. Often, she felt afraid because so much was unfamiliar, yet she was determined to continue so that she could orientate herself. If she could actually understand what was going on, she would be able to make more informed choices.

Suddenly she saw a large, old house. It was very tall, with many storeys. As the girl looked upwards, she saw that the house was full of drunk people who looked like wolves. They laughed, full of bravado, hanging out of the windows. As she got nearer, still undetected, she managed to snatch a glance through the curtains. Inside was a throne room and banquet hall where obscene scenes and rituals were taking place behind closed doors.

The girl was overcome with horror, and was just about to scream, but she realized in a split second that this would betray her presence. Instead, she ran away and watched the house from a distance. It was then that she saw a bauble of very strong light situated right on top of the roof, as if it was observing and monitoring all this from an upper standpoint. The light flashed on and off like the warning lights of an ambulance. It was on highest alert and waiting for the right moment to strike.

And strike it did. A concentrated beam of light, like lightening from heaven, split the house to the very core, revealing depravity and corruption. The beam of light tried to spin. At first, this was difficult due to the "dark" atmosphere in the house, but it soon got up speed and turned into a gyrating tornado which swallowed everything in its path. Soon, the tall house was consumed by fire.

The girl watched with amazement as this unstoppable cleansing process took place, but although the fire cast huge shadows and sparks across the city, most people ignored it and continued going about their daily business. Sometimes a spark from the fire would land in a nearby street, and a fire brigade would be called to put it out. Thus, the temporary emergency was dealt with, without any knowledge of the towering inferno next door. Most people simply did not lift their heads, and they shut out any unusual sounds.

Some people eventually realized that something was wrong, and began to write down notes about their observations. Some were convinced that the fire was divine, and they threw themselves into it. Others locked themselves into their houses. Others flung themselves onto the ground and asked forgiveness. Others crowded into churches and felt helpless. These people sensed that they were living in end times, and everyone dealt with that in different ways.

A few people were determined to get a bigger picture of what was really going on, and they climbed to the top of towers and tall buildings to survey the city which was laid out like a map below. From this position, they could see the progress of the tornado. They saw that some buildings were torched, and they saw that other areas remained untouched. They concluded that this was not the way in which a tornado would usually travel, and it was not the way in which fire would usually spread. As they looked out over the city lying like a map before them, they suddenly saw a pair of very large hands, holding the map. And in this instant, they realized that the city was IN DIVINE HANDS and that all processes were being conducted in compassion and FOR THE BENEFIT OF ALL.

THE ROUNDABOUT

Imagine you are a small child who sees a roundabout for the very first time. You will mount a wooden horse with innocent delight, anticipating that something wonderful is going to happen. Then you are warned that the roundabout will start, and you are filled with trepidation. You may be shocked at the sudden movement and at the pace which is much faster than you expected, but you gradually get used to it - or conceal your fear - accepting it as "normal". Your fear may also be assuaged by your waving smiling parents shouting words of encouragement as you fleetingly pass them by.

As a small child, everything is all right, despite fear, if those parents remain in their places. If they depart for a minute or two, your world falls apart until they reappear. This is where FAMILIARITY plays a significant role. Even if there are many patches of unfamiliar ground between the rotations of the roundabout, recognising landmarks bolsters your confidence that you know where you are in the world. This is your reality, your family, your framework in which you comfortably reside, inside the comfort zone.

If you fly past other zones at great speed, barely skimming the surface as you scan the landscape for recognisable landmarks, you will actually FAIL TO PENETRATE THE SURFACE. YOU WILL NOT REALISE THAT THIS IS A MUCH MORE VIBRANT, CONFUSING, COMPLEX AND DISTURBING WORLD than you can imagine.

If you travel through this "world" full of dense lies and corruption, you will also encounter the opposite - delights which stretch far beyond your physical senses, your imagination and your presently closeted planet. If you do this, YOU WILL ALSO DISCOVER YOUR REAL SELVES - WHERE YOU HAVE COMPROMISED, WHAT YOU HAVE TOLERATED, AND WHERE YOU HAVE DISTRIBUTED FALSE AND INAPPROPRIATE PRAISE.

The feeling of flying directionless through life, swinging past seemingly unfamiliar, irrelevant and vaguely unpleasant scenery, WILL CEASE, BECAUSE ALL ROUNDABOUTS WILL SUDDENLY STOP, AND YOU WILL BE ABLE TO SEE YOUR SURROUNDINGS WITH ABSOLUTE CLARITY AND IMMEDIACY. You will be forced to descend from your pedestals and your proud horses, and descend into the mire, as well as the joy, of what you have collectively produced. The only travelling, now, will not be circular or linear, but a movement involving depth and lateral thinking, involving ALL-EMCOMPASSING PERSPEC-TIVES. You will walk round the roundabout, taking time to discover what you overlooked and what you missed out on as you were spinning so quickly for the thrill of it. Ask yourselves why you need this furious pace in your lives, this instant gratification, this constant distraction from the truth which is so near, if only you will step down and examine it.

The period of nothingness, of no travel, of "no time" and no distractions approaches. Prepare yourselves well, for the task is formidable, the grief is great, and the ensuing joy and relief unfathomable. Reset your rapid swirling movements to nought. Return to stillness, to your centre of Godliness which is the pivot of the roundabout, reconnecting your cord to Creation, whose laws have been so sadly broken.

THE CELESTIAL CLEARING HOUSE

The huge river flows through a CELESTIAL CLEARING HOUSE, before it joins the sea. Fish who are incapable of swimming for long periods without seeing their destination or a shore in the distance, are taken out before they reach the expanses of the great ocean of the universe.

Those who have never looked forward in anticipation of something beyond their comprehension are carefully removed, because they would not survive the shock of the horizon of infinity. They must first experience a "safer haven", in preparation for open seas.

Some fish struggle to follow their own particular paths, despite strong currents. They continue undeterred, despite adversity, faring well on their journeys. If these fish are presented with the sight of endless waters, they are not devastated or overwhelmed. They possess the initiative and presence of mind to turn around and make for new shores.

Timid fish, who have bunched together in a protective group, will discover that their particular group belief is not an important factor in the clearing-house. Here, everyone is an individual with a unique history based on a multitude of individual decisions. In the clearing house, these fish are separated from their group identity, and are examined in view of their individual choices.

Those fish who have always "gone with the flow" without question, without contemplation, without inward reflection, cannot continue in the same manner. They are forced to pause and take a stand. They are asked to reflect upon their decision not to question the flow, or to examine it.

To allow these into the ocean would be subjecting them to even more powerful tides and waves - to the immense power of the seas which would batter and destroy them. They too are invited to go elsewhere, or turn the corner, or enter a period of thoughtful stillness, of non-movement, to realise where they are and where they want to be.

Every fish goes through this process, choosing the next door, into the next experience, or into the next life. This process involves a period of pause in the clearing house, where all are sorted in conjunction with their own will, whether consciously or subconsciously.

The fish which have sometimes dared to face the current, will have developed the strength and self-determination to face the future fearlessly and honestly. They are the ones who CAN question the usual flow, who have developed personal qualities of self-reliance and discernment, and who have conducted thorough and honest investigation. They are the ones who can withstand the glory of the open seas.

CHAPTER 9

PARABLES WHICH STRENGTHEN OUR INTERCONNECTION

THE WATCHER OF THE WORLD

Imagine you are sitting alone at the edge of a lake, wearing robes of white which sparkle with glints of silver. You are intensely aware of everything around you. You sit there throughout the seasons, watching shades of vegetation, sky and water change, while the contours remain largely the same. Sometimes the surface of the lake is roughly textured, and at other times it is as still as glass, and then you can see a clump of white waterlilies floating in the centre.

Your hearing is acute. In autumn, you hear the fall of every dry, crackling leaf. In winter, you hear the pieces of broken ice chiming like small bells as they hit the shoreline. In spring, you note the tiny scurrying feet of awakened animals in search for food. In summer, you send love and energy to the white lilies in the lake, and you listen to the wind which carries the sound of flutes and drums from a nearby village, whenever celebrations are taking place.

The reason for sitting so still during these passing seasons is very clear to you: you know that EVERY MOVE YOU MAKE CAN BE FELT BY SOMEONE ELSE. Whenever you think of a place or person, a silver thread immediately emerges from your forehead and travels to that person, attaching itself to them. Your fingers are attached by silver threads to everything you have ever touched.

And so, you sit there in total stillness, for uncontrolled movement would cause chaos. Instead, you concentrate on the MOVE-MENT WITHIN.

After some deliberation, you are inspired to select a stone, half white and half black, and throw it into the lake. It takes you a very long time to select the right stone, weighing and turning each one slowly in your hand to check their smooth surfaces for flaws.

Some are white marble stones veined with black. Some are jet black stones speckled with white. When you find the perfect stone, balanced in shape and colour, you bless it and say MAY MY ACTION CAUSE THE HEAVENS TO OPEN FOR THOSE EYES WHICH DO NOT SEE. One calm, summer's day, when the water is as motionless as a mirror, you throw it into the lake.

When the stone hits the surface of the water, ripples emanate, and just as you are connected by threads to everything you have touched, you are also connected to all movement you have caused. You watch and feel the ripples gathering momentum as you follow them with your eyes, as if the ripples are your finger-tips stretching into unknown realms. When they reach the middle of the lake where the white waterlilies grow, the force is so great that the lilies are swept away. As the water carries the lilies to-wards the shore, you feel the absolute purity of the flowers reso-nating in your heart.

Small children playing on the shores of the lake look up in wonder to see the white flowers arriving at the water's edge. Uncon-sciously, their own purity resonates with the purity of the flowers, and so they are automatically drawn towards them. The children gather them joyfully in their arms and bring them home to their parents. In the darkness of those small simple homes, the flowers emit a sort of ethereal light, acting as a lamp which illuminates the shadows.

They discover that when a white flower is placed near an ailing person, the patient will recover. And so, the flowers are greatly desired and highly prized. Many flowers are jealously guarded until they eventually wither and die. Some are preserved as holy relics, but then they lose their power.

There are some people, however, who do not keep the flowers for themselves alone. They feel that this wonder should be shared, so secretly they take the flowers to troubled lands where darkness reigns. Some distribute them petal by petal to poor beggar children. Some decide to plant the flowers into the ground in a secret and secluded place. They sit round the plant in a circle, sending it all their love and energy so that it might take root and grow well. Then they build a wall around the plant so that it might not be discovered.

Later the wall is torn down by marauders, but the bush does not die completely, and a woman secretly takes the seeds and plants them in a distant forest. Here she sits and watches until they take root. Here they flourish in seclusion until one day, trees of white flowers poke their head high above the horizon.

All this YOU CAN SEE, as you sit timelessly and motionlessly at the lakeside, growing older and weaker. The flowers have travelled in a complete circle round the globe. The trees with the white flowers are growing in the forest behind you. You cannot see them with your physical eyes, but I you can feel the connection through the silver threads attached to your fingers. In the background, you can again hear the sound of musical instruments in a village celebration.

When they suddenly stop, you know that the villagers have noticed the new white trees and are walking towards them with wonder. They have heard many old stories about these healing flowers, and they see that a silver thread runs from the trees across the forest floor, across the meadows, towards the lakeside where you sit.

The villagers are astonished to discover you there, with silver cords stretching from your body in all directions. They think you are some sort of god or goddess, and they begin to cry and bow down, but you motion to them to stop. You tell them that they can also generate healing and high levels of awareness, if they look upwards. On doing so, they see the FIRST SILVER THREAD OF ALL – THEIR VERY OWN CELESTIAL CONNECTION TO THE DIVINE CREATOR. You tell them they can invite this thread into their lives, if they so desire. Some accept this offer with great joy and take up sitting positions on the edge of the lake, seemingly motionless but growing inwardly. They, in their turn, become a WATCHER OF THE WORLD, acutely aware of their every thought and movement, and the consequences thereof.

THE JIGSAW PUZZLE ORGANISED BY THE DIVINE

Hands belonging to a huge celestial being emptied a box of puzzle pieces (WHICH ALL CAME FROM THE SAME SOURCE) onto a table. The pieces were scattered far and wide. Some were face up. Others were face down. First of all, the celestial hands ensured that all the pieces were face up. They were all counted, and none was found missing, so the celestial being departed in the confident knowledge that he had initiated the process of "coming together", and that all pieces were perfect. He knew that each piece was unique and essential to the whole. And he knew that if the pieces rearranged themselves, the full picture would come into view.

Each piece actually represented one inhabitant on earth. Through inner decisions and outer movements, each person would find their perfect position, thus contributing to a harmonious and completed whole. The pieces wandered around on the table, as if wandering through life, looking for a sign that they were going in the right direction. Sometimes a flash of colour or an attractive shape would compass their direction. When pieces of the same colour or pattern met as a group, there was great excitement, as they knew that they belonged together somehow.

And so, all pieces were on an individual journey, with a view to finding others in alignment with themselves.

Sometimes the celestial being would come back to observe whether the jigsaw was being put together. If he saw a piece wandering off by itself, or approaching danger (the edge of the table), he would turn it around, to give it a new perspective. In very difficult cases, he would actually pluck the piece from the table and position it exactly where it was supposed to be. This was a shock for the piece, but necessary.

If the celestial being saw a piece which was very sad, and which had given up its search, then he would send a "neighbouring" piece in their direction to console and inspire. Much joy arose when two pieces found that they fitted together perfectly in both shape and colour. Then they interlocked, as jigsaw pieces do, and continued their search for more interlocking parts.

This process of looking for those of similar mind and intention, recognising friends and joining forces, was approved by the watching celestial eyes. Some pieces, however, did not take part at all. They became more and more isolated, but however long this took, the celestial being repeatedly pushed them gently but firmly in new directions.

In the end, only one piece was missing for the completion of the picture. The missing piece did not actually need to search very hard, for his final destination was all too clear. After refusing to participate for so long, it was very difficult for this piece to surrender to the will of the celestial being and join his fellows, but he had to swallow his pride and do so.

When the puzzle was complete, the celestial being addressed the pieces in a grave voice: "Dear friends on earth: you are ALL involved with the effort to UPLIFT YOUR EARTH AT THIS TIME.

YOU ARE A UNIQUE AND ESSENTIAL PART OF THE SUP-
PORTING STRUCTURE, AND YOU HAVE COME INTO THE
KNOWING OF YOUR CORRECT POSITION AND YOUR
GREAT INDIVIDUAL AND COLLECTIVE RESPONSIBILITY.
We congratulate you on your achievement. All pieces are present
and perfectly matched. Thus you can move forward, united AS
ONE."

LIFE IN THE HOTHOUSE

Imagine yourselves as plants, growing as tender seedlings, receiving nurture each day from the sun and rain, and also inde-
pendently drawing your own nourishment from the abundant soil,
automatically stretching towards the light, growing tall yet developing stability simultaneously through your roots in the earth.

Until one day the delicate tendrils of your exploring roots strike
something hard. Your attention is diverted from the light, distracted and frustrated by this unseen barrier. It appears to be im-
movable, so you adapt, and your roots grow further, but they are
programmed to grow in a different direction.

This experience is repeated, and in the end, all your roots meet
and are so densely meshed that there is no longer any soil or
nourishment between them. Growth has stopped. You are en-
tirely dependent on what you receive from above.

It is at this point that you may realise that you are a prisoner. You
are a pot plant in a hothouse, as opposed to a seedling in the
forest. You are contained. Your growth is contained. Your potential for huge and spectacular growth is contained.

STUNTED GROWTH, YOUR LONELINESS, YOUR FEELINGS OF SEPARATION, YOUR NARROW VIEWS AND EXPERIENCES, YOUR LIMITIED PERCEPTIONS AND SELF-CENTRED BIGOTTED VIEWS ARE ALL DERIVED FROM YOUR VOLUNTARY DECISION TO GROW IN A LIMITING ENVIRONMENT WHICH REDUCES YOU TO SMALL, POWERLESS AND ULTIMATELY CONTROLLABLE ENTITIES.

IN THIS CONDITION, YOU WILL NEVER EXPERIENCE TRUE CONTACT WITH OTHERS OR DEVELOP NETWORKS OF UNITY.

Your compartmentalisations into different racial, religious, social, intellectual and financial POTS blind you to the basic concept of yourselves as constantly growing and evolving beings working together for the glory of your common good, and for the glory of your DIVINE PARENTS whose watchful eyes never stray from your side, observing their children's choices.

REMOVE YOURSELVES FROM YOUR PRISONS OF MIND AND MOVE INTO ONENESS. For soon shall all artificial walls of this nature fall in one abrupt episode, enabling communication and touch and contact BETWEEN ALL.

How will you react? Will your long years as members of this or that section of society or religion or country PREVENT YOU FROM MOVING ON, EVEN THOUGH THE WALLS HAVE BEEN REMOVED?

It is time to disregard that which separates you and focus on the COMMON DENOMINATORS which link you for eternity, for this will bring you new worlds and great joy.

116

THE VOYAGE OF THE SHIP OF UNITY

Many ships of different sizes were crossing a very choppy ocean in roughly the same direction, heading for a beautiful island far away in the distance. They had heard that the island was like paradise, so this was their goal.

Some ships were more like boats - small and open. The passengers sat silently with their heads bowed, or they chanted low incantations or mantras. They were mostly in fear, not daring to look up, although they were very aware of the large waves, and there was great tension in their bodies.

One ship was very large, carrying a great number of soldiers in uniform, accompanied by families who said very little and who did as was expected of them. A brass band was playing triumphant music, and this was accompanied by flag hoisting, followed by speeches. The ship was big and powerful. No-one really noticed the size of the waves at all because their attention was focused elsewhere.

On a large cruise ship, everyone was on the party deck, dancing and drinking, so they did not notice the waves either. If they fell over, they put it down to their alcohol intake. In the end, the drunk captain put the ship on automatic, and everyone fell asleep.

On one of the smaller ships, the SHIP OF UNITY, the passengers were all alert. They were well organised, helped each other, and showed understanding in all difficult circumstances. Those who were afraid were comforted, those who were hungry were fed. The children were told stories and the old were cared for. It was clear that they had to weather this ordeal together, as there was no option of leaving the ship. There were always at least two lookouts at the prow of the ship, scouring the horizon for danger, and watching the water for rocks. They all worked in unison and communicated frequently.

Suddenly the storm worsened, and the view of the island in the distance was completely blocked. It was almost as if a bank of solid mist had descended, except that this was actually a row of swirling whirlwinds. There was only just enough room to pass between the whirlwinds, and this clearly had to be very carefully navigated and could only be achieved through joint effort.

The look-outs on the SHIP OF UNITY immediately saw the whirlwinds and sounded the alarm by ringing bells. They held themselves in a state of readiness while continuing to attend to everyone's basic needs. But the people in the other ships did not hear the bells. The brass band on the military ship drowned the sound of the alarm. The passengers on the small boats heard the alarm, but ignored it out of fear, bending their heads even more fervently in prayer, begging to be saved. And the others heard nothing because they were asleep.

This meant that the majority of boats simply continued to steer directly for the whirlwinds and were caught up by them. They were held there by a strong force, as if captured within a magnetic field. Only the SHIP OF UNITY managed to avoid the whirlwinds. As they looked back, they saw the other ships twirling slowly. They felt great sorrow, as they felt they had not managed to warn them, but they knew also that they had done their best.

When the ship reached the shores of the beautiful island, everyone cried and fell onto the sandy shore, relieved that the journey was over. Their emotions, which had been largely kept under wraps during the journey, were now all released. They seemed, now, to have a new perspective and a new way of seeing.

When the survivors turned around to look at the whirlwinds, they saw that they were actually great, lighted beings deliberately whipping up the winds to test incoming ships. The number of ships now approaching was huge, and the lighted beings had an enormous task. The people on shore understood that they had passed this test, and that they were now to proceed down a path into the forest. This path was lined by more angels, bowing in acknowledgement of their achievement. At the end of the path was the largest lighted being of all, who embraced everyone in turn and brought them all to a place of rest to recover from their experience.

CHAPTER 10

PARABLES WHICH INSPIRE OPTIMISM AND EVOKE JOY

THE FISH THAT SWAM VERTICALLY

Once upon a time there was a very deep ocean floor. It was so deep, in fact, that no light shed through to the bottom. A very large fish appeared. Like all fish at this depth, it was luminous and looked rather ghostly and aggressive. Then a small fish arrived. Both fish looked each other in the eye and bared their teeth, expecting a fight, preparing to defend themselves. The fish swam around each other tentatively, and then the smaller fish eventually retreated, feeling fear but not showing it, retiring to the depths of the ocean.

The smaller fish spent a lot of time hiding in holes between the coral. Whenever he ventured out into the open, he kept a sharp lookout for other fish. But he was happiest hiding, as it was a great strain to have to remain aware all the time. And because all predators were luminous, the small fish learnt to associate light with danger.

One day the fish looked out of his hole to see a vertical beam of light landing in a circle on the ocean floor. The beam appeared to be never-ending, stretching upwards through the water. Initially, the fish was afraid and suspicious. It had never seen such a strong light before, but eventually it overcame its fright and ventured out, mostly because his life in the hole was pretty safe, but also pretty boring.

The fish carefully swam up to the beam of light to investigate. The nearer it got, the warmer he felt, and this was a sort of pleasant warmth which made him feel happy. Still, there was a part of him which thought THIS MAY BE A TRICK. In the end, curiosity got the better of him, and he stuck his nose into the light beam, anticipating a shock of some sort, but instead, the fish felt a surge of energy.

Thus, the little fish discovered that the light was not an unpleasant luminous creature, but something ethereal and transparent. The fish was still a little worried, swimming in and out of the light to test it out. When all his fear was lost, and in a final SUPREME MOMENT OF RELEASE AND SURRENDER, the fish entered the beam and swam upwards, vertically, constantly showered with light, until he reached the very surface of the ocean. At that point, the fish leapt into the sunlight which was much more radiant and brighter than his wildest imaginings.

JOURNEY TO THE SOURCE

A long procession of people in brown hooded robes was journeying on foot over the floor of a very narrow valley with steep sides. The people knew that this journey would end soon, in fact there was no way out of this enclosed valley: it came to an abrupt end at a sheer face of rock, over which poured a high waterfall.

Along the way, riders on white horses offered their services to the wanderers, offering them rides so that they would reach their destination earlier, but most of the wanderers were steadfast, knowing in their hearts that every step was important, and that short-cuts also cut short the learning process. Thus, they continued to walk, learning how to live and camp together.

Their hope of actually reaching a "destination" was sometimes very low. On such occasions, some of them complained and displayed impatience, while others remained silent and sought stillness, listening for the strange and sporadic creaking sound which originated somewhere in the distance, and which echoed softly round the valley. This sound gave them comfort, for it suggested that there was SO MUCH MORE THAN THAT WHICH THEY

PRESENTLY PERCEIVED FROM THEIR LIMITED POINT OF VISION.

Others were inspired to DIG DEEPER INTERNALLY AND EX-TERNALLY. When they dug into the ground, they discovered nuggets of orange gold beneath the soil. These could not be removed, however. They were somehow fixed. And through this, the wanderers were reminded of the TREASURES UNSEEN AND IMMOVEABLE, YET TO BE REVEALED, BUT ALWAYS IN EXISTENCE BENEATH THE SHROUD OF DARKNESS.

When the travellers reached the end of the valley, they were forced to stop and set up camp. The water from the waterfall was their only sustenance. Those with enough stamina and curiosity continued, and they discovered a very steep, narrow path, cut into the rock. It led upwards, winding on to the top of the waterfall.

At the top of the waterfall, the resilient wanderers discovered a lush plateau of fields surrounding a large lake. Food was abundant. The meadows were populated by smiling, dancing people who welcomed them, and who directed them towards a huge tree. This tree was hundreds of years old, with a startlingly thick trunk, but its most astonishing feature was that it was made of solid gold. It was then that the adventurous wanderers recognised this tree as the MOTHER who had birthed the gold nuggets which had inspired them during their journey through the valley. A split second later, the wanderers intuitively realised that the nuggets they had seen were actually orange roots. THE ROOTS HAD GROWN THROUGH THE THICKEST OF ROCK AND THE THINEST OF SOIL.

A huge swing was attached to the tree. An angel sat on the swing, and as it moved to and fro, the wanderers recognised the creaking of the branches – the noise which they had heard in the valley below. Seeing the travellers arrive, the angel jumped off the swing and welcomed them saying NOW THERE IS NO NEED TO TRANSPORT TO YOUR EARS THE SOUND OF OUR DIVINE MOVEMENTS, BECAUSE NOW YOU CAN SEE THE SOURCE WHICH CREATES THE MOTION AND THE SOUND.

The travellers were overcome that they had reached the end of their journey, though they understood that this was just the beginning: THEY THEMSELVES WOULD NOW MAKE THEMSELVES HEARD, GIVING CLUES AND INSPIRATION TO OTHERS, SO THAT THEY WOULD SIMILARLY FOLLOW THE CLUES TO FIND THE SOURCE – a place of perfect shelter, calm and love.

THE BOOK OF LIFE

A very large book appeared in front of a pale, thin woman. It was the book of her life, and it was opened at the middle. The page on the left said PAST in large letters, and the page on the right said FUTURE. The woman sat on the crack between past and future, in the middle of the book.

Her body was not solid. One by one the pages of the past turned, cutting through her almost as if she was invisible. As the pages turned, they sieved fear, sorrow and anger out of the body of the woman. These black blotches were related to unpleasant past events in her life, and now appeared on the pages which had passed through her. After this residue from the past had been TAKEN OUT OF HER BODY, it became more porous and lighter.

Then the pages of the future started to turn, one by one, again cutting through the woman's body. Again, unhealthy elements were taken out of her body. These were all anticipations, expectations and pressures which clouded her potential for the future. With each page that turned, her body became lighter, and in the end her skin was completely transparent and consisted of finely meshed netting which let everything through. It was COMPLETELY FLEXIBLE, COMPLETELY READY TO ABSORB WHATEVER CAME. IT WAS READY TO DISPERSE THE OLD IMMEDIATELY, AND TO WELCOME THE NEW WITHOUT HESITATION.

THE LEAP OF FAITH

A small, chubby boy was sitting on the grass, staring unhappily at the ground. Ladies dressed in long, white robes were looking after him and a lot of other children. A big box of fancy dress clothing stood in the middle of the field, and the children screamed with excitement as they discovered a huge variety of costumes, each more elaborate and beautiful than the next.

When they found a suit that fit, they took on that particular role, pretending to be birds, fairies, elves or butterflies. One of the ladies tried to animate the little chubby boy, showing him gorgeous costumes, but he was too sad to make much of an effort, and just sat watching.

Suddenly, one of the white ladies produced a large hoop and positioned it vertically on the grass, as if someone was going to jump through it. The costumed children ran towards it excitedly but stopped in surprise when they looked through the hoop. On the other side, instead of grass, was nothing except for a black hole.

The lady in white encouraged the children gently, saying that if they dared to go through the hoop, their dreams would come true. She told them that something was on the other side, even though they could not see it.

The first child plucked up his courage and went through the hoop. He disappeared completely. But the children could hear his excited cries on the "other side" saying "I am flying! I am a bird!"

One by one, they followed him through the hoop. The small, sad, chubby boy became even sadder, because all the other children were gone – they always came and went, never staying for long.

Then the lady in white carried the small boy to the edge of the hoop and whispered in his ear: "You cannot see the other side, BUT KNOW THAT IT IS THERE". Then she went through the hoop herself and disappeared into the darkness.

Now the little boy was very distraught because he was completely alone. But then he heard the voice of the lady in white, his guardian angel, encouraging him to take this leap of faith. When he did so, she caught him joyfully in her arms and threw him up into the sky because there, on the other side, everyone was able to fly.

The small boy smiled and rejoiced, and the next time he saw a hoop being set up, he was always one of those who dared to jump through it, not knowing what his next experience might be, but knowing he would always learn something new, and knowing that his guardian angel would always be waiting to catch him the moment he jumped into the unknown.

THE END OF "WAIT AND SEE"

A woman was sitting on a plain wooden chair in the middle of the desert. Her gaze was fixed on the very dry sand, watching intently for any sign of life, scouring every inch to see if little green shoots were emerging from the ground.

She knew that the sand contained seeds, because she had the vague memory of sewing them there herself. But she was rather despondent because nothing could be seen.

However, she KNEW in her subconscious that the seeds had potential, and that they must be developing a root system underground, beyond her present sight.

To counteract her despondency, she tore her eyes away from the sand and looked up to gain another perspective. There, in the very far distance, she saw a number of dark clouds on the horizon. This ignited her joy. She now knew, beyond a shadow of doubt, that rain was approaching, and that she would witness the growth of the seeds.

Feelings of doubt only resurfaced whenever she returned to prolonged, studied contemplation of the empty desert. The woman learned that it was better to gaze at the horizon at frequent intervals, and thus she was able to keep her mental balance and focus during that very long period of time during which the black clouds very slowly drifted towards her.

The arrival of flocks of birds on the parched soil, some white and some black, reassured the woman that she had indeed sewn seeds there in the very distant past. The birds tried to find the seeds, and squabbled among themselves, but they did not find them because they were so deep below the surface.

The inevitable happened. The rain began to fall, and the seeds grew rapidly into seedlings. Soon they grew into plants and bushes laden with flowers and fruit, as they were programmed to do.

The chair the woman was sitting on started to sink into the rain-soaked ground, and thus she realised that it was time to move on. She carried the chair through the lush field she had created, and entered another desert. Here, she dug deep holes and put a seed into each one. Then she sat down on her chair, wondering what would happen this time.

After contemplation, she realised that whatever happened, this was not a question of "wait and see", but the result of her own actions and expectations, and she was filled with the knowledge and joy of her own creativity.

She realised that she did not need to stay on the chair and wait. She realised that the seeds would germinate by themselves WHEN THE TIME WAS RIPE AND WHEN THE CONDITIONS WERE PERFECT.

Again, a flock of birds appeared. This time, all the birds were grey. They no longer fought with each other. Similarly, the woman's gaze was no longer torn between watching the sand and scouring the horizon. And so she left and continued her journey, knowing that her energy was no longer needed in that particular area of desert.

CROSSING THE BATTLEFIELD

A white horse was walking around slowly and clumsily in a black field, up to his ankles in mud. He felt weighed down and lethargic. He looked down continuously at the sticky, dark mud, wondering how he might be rid of it.

Raising his head, the horse saw a red field nearby, where there seemed to be whole group of horses and a lot more action, and so he dragged himself in that direction. When he arrived, the horse found himself on a battlefield, surrounded by conflict and blood. While traversing this field, he encountered many difficulties trying to prevent getting wounded and getting involved.

On the other side of the battlefield was a very small white path with thorns on either side, in fact the entrance was almost invisible, but by this time the once lethargic horse was very much awake and it immediately caught his attention. It did not promise much, but it seemed to the horse that this was the only route of escape. Once on this path – which was extremely narrow - the horse initially had difficulty staying his course, and was scratched by thorns and threatened by wild animals on every side. But in spite of this, he knew he was safe on the white path and that the wild animals could not hurt him unless he wandered off it.

With increasing confidence that this was the right way to go, the white horse relaxed and broke into a trot. The more relaxed he became, the more the path widened, and now the wild animals were so far away that the horse did not give them a second thought. The path ended on a white shoreline, with the sea behind it. The horse entered the sea joyfully to be completely cleansed and to re-join a multitude of other horses who had also found their way there.

THE VALE OF TEARS

A young girl stood in a desert on a huge dome of sand, surveying the absolute barrenness of the earth. In her mind's eye, she remembered scenes of terrible destruction and desecration in her life, lamenting all situations involving war, famine, chaos and distress. And through all this, she had kept a stiff upper lip. She had even retained a slight smile on her strained face in the hope that this would somehow ward off what she considered "evil".

But now she stood on the huge sand dome overlooking the desert. The smile was gone and her eyes brimmed with tears. SHE HAD NEVER CRIED BEFORE. There was nothing here but wind, sand and the white bones of dead camels.

As the wind grew stronger she noticed a few clumps of dead twigs being blown across the desert, and at this point she burst into uncontrollable sobs. She walked on and on, blinded by her own tears, until she reached the very edge of the desert. Here she was greeted by a row of angelic beings who stood in her path. They stopped her gently and motioned to her to turn around.

To her great amazement, the desert was suddenly full of flowers. The small clumps of twigs were actually plants which had purposely uprooted themselves and formed ball-like shapes so that their seeds – still fastened to the twigs – had a better chance of rolling to fertile ground. The many tears shed by the girl had watered the seeds.

It was then that the girl realised the great power of the emotions which she had kept inside her for so long. She rejoiced in the desert garden, her new home, renamed THE VALE OF TEARS, and she laughed and cried there all day long, giving full expression to her deepest feelings, knowing that her authentic behaviour was benefitting all.

DREAM OF THE PERFECT COMMUNITY

A man woke up suddenly from a wonderful dream. He was sitting on the back of an enormous bird and was approaching a small village, regarding it from a great height. Moving over snow-covered country towards lush green countryside, he suddenly saw a glinting, round structure below. It sparkled as if gold was somehow built into the walls.

On landing and on closer inspection, the walls of the "houses" were made of stone and large expanses of glass, combining a rural look with high technology. The circular shape which he had seen from above actually included several households belonging to large families, similar to the way large family clans lived together in linked courtyards in ancient China. In the middle was a small, circular amphitheatre for meetings and celebrations.

It seemed to be the beginning of a new era: everyone, regardless of age or stature, collected here and went onto the amphitheatre stage, one by one. They introduced themselves, listed their skills and stated their mission in this new society.

Some were quite at ease in this situation, and others felt very shy, but in the end even the very youngest of souls went through this process. This allowed everyone to feel included, to be a part of the community which was trying to regulate and organise itself in a new, sustainable and humanitarian way. This stating of skills enabled the development of small groups with similar interests and capabilities. Everyone talked simply and honestly and put their hand on their heart as they did so.

The central "circle" or island was residential only, surrounded by a wall so that small children could run around safely and unhindered, and beyond that lay a moat with several stone bridges crossing over into the next "circle".

The second circle, which enclosed the first circle, included schools and areas for agricultural, creative and organisational pursuits. Beyond this was the third circle which was used for trading, public meetings, and interaction. The third circle actually intersected with the third circle of neighbouring communities.

In the mornings, everyone was wakened by gentle, live music. Breakfast was taken altogether in the central open space, after which everyone proceeded to their own particular task.

At 12.00 midday, bells rang and everyone stopped their activities immediately, standing in silent devotion and communion with Source, facing the island and blessing their homes and families. Then they turned outwards to bless their neighbours and the rest of their world.

In the evenings, the community met to sit together, talk and exchange ideas. In the course of their discussions, decisions were taken to form sanctuaries where all animals were well treated and loved. No-one ate meat any more.

Appraisal was made of all available resources, and new rubbish control and dispersal systems were introduced. Collecting points were set up for surplus machinery, tools, seeds and even clothes. These were distributed to whoever needed them, and then returned if no longer needed.

Every evening programme also included quiet meditation time or listening to musical performances by local residents, including children.

Small workshops offering emotional release through dance and body work were a constant daily feature because so much trauma and readjustment was taking place. Lectures were given to fill out the missing history of the planet and the universe.

There was no more noise, as cars and planes were trappings of the past. They were replaced by a completely different hovering transit system. All the roads were transformed into gardens and vegetable patches. As the climate was steady, continuously warm and agreeable, there was no need to wear shoes any more.

There were no more solitary individuals, only large communities which met regularly, so there was much less need for phones or other communication media. Misunderstandings generally did not arise as there was so much personal contact, and there was always someone to consult if problems arose. There was no such thing as a busy social schedule or a packed timetable. Everything was measured and balanced.

After deep reflection, the man came to the conclusion that the dream was trying to convey the following: IT IS OUR RESPON-SIBILITY TO CARRY PICTURES OF IDEAL LIVING AND WORKING CONDITIONS IN OUR MINDS, FOR THIS WILL PROMOTE AND FACILITATE THEIR CONSTRUCTION IN THE FUTURE. WE SHOULD DARE TO CREATE THE VERY BEST FOR OURSELVES AND OTHERS. WE SHOULD ASSUME LEADERSHIP AND COUNTERACT THE DISHARMONY AND REGRESSION IN SOCIETY. WE SHOULD STRIVE, ALWAYS, TO MANIFEST THE DIVINE, AND TO TURN ALL EARTH INTO A GARDEN.

Rosie Jackson is an author, artist, composer and founder of THE SPIRITUAL REVOLUTION PROJECT. This encompasses all aspects of her work – paintings, music, videos, books and seminars to develop self-awareness. Teaching spiritual principles in order to promote consciousness, her music and art are powerful catalysts of spiritual uplift.

She is inventor of THE UNITY TAROT which documents the transformation of 100 global villagers in two very large paintings, and in 100 written biographies. This serves as a framework for her seminars, both local and international.

Since 2010, Rosie Jackson has been receiving telepathic messages and visions from the angel, Seraphin. These communications urge us to protect our earth and show how paradise on earth can be achieved. The messages are presently available in English, German, Italian, Spanish, Dutch and Korean.

Born and educated in England, Rosie Jackson studied German and French and qualified as a teacher. She has worked as a teaching instructor in China, and as translator, designer and editor for various publishing houses in Europe. She has also translated professionally for large companies.

She now works freelance near Munich, Germany, and in Liguria, Italy. She offers spiritual counselling sessions and can be reached under rosie@rosiejackson.de.

WORKS BY ROSIE JACKSON

Compilations of Seraphin Messages in English, German, Italian
Dutch and Spanish, from 2010 to 2019
The Unity Tarot in English and German, Parts 1 and 2
The Seraphin Prophecies and *Mediation Visions*
(These can be downloaded at
http://www.rosie-jackson.de/pages/e_links.html)

OTHERS PUBLICATIONS BY ROSIE JACKSON

Seraphin's Spirituality School
    ISBN 978-3-749485-84-0
*The Absolutely Amazing Activity Book of Snakes, Stars and
    Snowballs.* ISBN 978-3-8370-0238-6
Wie das Schweinchen Prinzessin Prunella das Lachen lernte
    ISBN 978-3-749428-85-4
Ich bin Lebendigkeit:
    Eine Reise zu mehr Authentizität, Kraft und Freude
    ISBN 978-3937883-32-8. EchnAton Publishers

ROSIE JACKSON: WEBSITES

ART: www.rosiejackson.de
SEMINARS:
http://www.rosie-jackson.de/revolution/Seminar_Termine.html
SERAPHIN MESSAGES:
www.rosiejackson.de/Seraphin
THE SPIRITUAL REVOLUTION PROJECT:
http://www.rosie-jackson.de/revolution/Projekt_und_Vision.html
YOUTUBE MUSIC/ART VIDEOS https://www.youtube.com/cha-
nel/UCMCeJnqJ9Y7hqAExYmm9iKA

Rosie Jackson

AN ANGEL SPEAKS

SERAPHIN'S SPIRITUALITY SCHOOL

YOUR DIVINE ROLE: CREATING AN ERA OF PEACE

ISBN 978-3-749485-84-0. 2019. 292 pages

Seraphin is an angel who send us messages of hope and inspiration, as well as advice and practical suggestions. Our world requires a drastic makeover, and this will be fueled by a universal change of heart, by widening our perspectives, and by reconnecting to the divine core within us, which impels us to develop our skills in service to humanity. Seraphin's statements provide remarkable insights, provoke intense reflection, and challenge our limited viewpoint. With great clarity, he points out the necessity for radical change, while knowing that we have the power to implement it. The messages in this book were received telepathically by author and artist , Rosie Jackson.

THE PURPOSE OF SERAPHIN'S SPIRITUALITY SCHOOL

This collection of 111 Seraphin Messages has 5 purposes. The first chapter, "Messages from the other side" encourage readers to start a writing journey, contacting unseen guides and "downloading" information relevant to your particular task on earth. As your spiritual abilities progress, you will increase in confidence, and you will become a source of inspiration for others.

Secondly, the chapters "Your divine purpose", "Transcending your past", "Creating your future", and "Your relationships", intend to further the reader's spiritual path, assisting them to develop potential, achieve excellency, and use these skills and knowledge for the benefit of all.

Chapter 3, "Preparing for transition", provides advice on how to deal with the intense times ahead. Due to our present position in the photon belt, our planet is showered with highly powered cosmic energies. These create enormous change, supporting everything of divine nature, and exposing that which is not.

Fourthly, the chapters on rebuilding our world offer instructions on how to address practical problems. They also highlight which qualities we should manifest in order to maintain peace, beauty and abundance on our world.

Fifthly, the goal of the very last chapter, "Reconnecting to the universe", aims to increase our awareness of our galactic neighbours who lovingly observe us. After millennia of "disconnection", we will finally resume our membership of the cosmic family.

YOU ARE IN SPIRITUALITY SCHOOL
Seraphin Message 253: Through Rosie, 29th January 2016

Despite the glory or the depravity of the physical surroundings in which you live, despite the physicality of your body and the need to attend to cleanliness and bodily functions, despite the physical motions you go through on a daily basis – all this is a MEANS TO EXPERIENCE rather than the AIM OF EXPERIENCE. If you are fixated on these, you will always be mentally leaning towards your next physical "fix", whether it be the next meal or the next massage or the next sporting event or the next piece of advice or the next sexual encounter. On the physical level, this is an endless series of events progressing in a linear fashion.

We ask you to consider that there is more to life than this, and in fact there is MORE LIFE in the sense that it does not simply stop after this incarnation.

If your mind is enslaved (and there are powers who would like to keep you in this position and who are very successful in their efforts to dupe you), if your mind is continually focusing on the next coffee, the next drug or entertainment slot, as in addiction, then there is NO ROOM FOR GROWTH. We do not mean growth in the physical sense but in the spiritual sense. Once deprived of your normal routine of "back to back" pleasures, as will surely come to pass in the next inevitable period of chaos on your world, you will be left with a VOID which you may be desperate to fill, or desperate to ignore.

To do so would be to deny your own growth as a divine being. To do so would be to reject the glory of choosing the much referenced and renowned "ETERNAL LIFE" (quoted in your holy books), offered to all who wish to climb the spiritual ladder. This is an offer to take part in the truly huge and organised undertaking which is the administration and development and improvement and growth and prosperity of the entire universe – a scenario still hidden from your present physical eyes, and yet you are part of it.

To repeat; you are not at a party, or on a battlefield, or in a playground, or in a one-time career; you are in a CLASSROOM. This life represents one class in an endless succession of educational institutions, whether on an evolutionary planet such as earth, whether on larger and more significant spheres, or beyond. Yet all experiences are significant and contribute to the WHOLE, including your experience HERE ON EARTH where so many detours and deviations from the DIVINE TEMPLATE have taken place.

Your physical experience is a challenge of how to find the divine in a quagmire of corruption and deception; and when you have discovered that uplifting factor which benefits ALL, it is your specific task to DEMONSTRATE THAT QUALITY, to RISE ABOVE THE PHYSICAL PLANE and to realise that you are both teacher and student in the UNIVERSAL SCHOOL OF SPIRITUALITY.

Rosie Jackson

THE ABSOLUTELY AMAZING ACTIVITY BOOK OF SNAKES, STARS AND SNOWBALLS

FURTHERING CREATIVE EXPRESSION
IN CHILDREN FROM THE AGE OF 7 UP

ISBN: 978-3-8370-0238-6

Each of these 80 pages presents a story, idea, or situation which stimulates children's imagination through questions, suggestions or invitations to wonder what happens next. The pictures they then draw are subconscious images of their inner world, feelings and desires, thus providing their carers with a valuable window to their soul. Once children are accustomed to expressing their own emotions and needs, they are better able to assess themselves and others on the path towards mutual understanding and peace. Like SNAKES they can shed their old skins, like SNOWBALLS they can move on and grow, reaching more and more towards the stars.